KU-198-881

the
canons
22

FYODOR DOSTOYEVSKY

Notes from Underground

Translated by
Natasha Randall

Introduction by
DBC Pierre

CANONGATE

Edinburgh · London

This new translation first published in Great Britain in 2012 by
Canongate Books Ltd, 14 High Street, Edinburgh EH1 1TE

www.canongate.tv

1

Translation copyright © Natasha Randall
Introduction copyright © DBC Pierre

The moral right of the translator has been asserted

British Library Cataloguing-in-Publication Data
A catalogue record for this book is available on
request from the British Library

ISBN 978 0 85786 021 7

Typeset in Goudy by Palimpsest Book Production Ltd,
Falkirk, Stirlingshire

Printed and bound by CPI Group (UK) Ltd, Croydon, CR0 4YY

INTRODUCTION

'But, it also seems to us that we may stop here.'

Picture the human zoo as a nervous system. Artists and thinkers drift to the nerve-endings, seeking answers in the sparks of single filaments, feeding back flickers in which we see ourselves across the complex, because we're connected, because even signals from the toes reflect us. Then a writer finds the brain-stem and sends ideas so central to who we are that they light the network at once and for ever.

That for me describes the scale of this little book.

I only want to spend a sentence on the story; you'll be there in a page or two anyway. Have no fear of too many surnames in a Russian salon – this is a bitter tirade by one spiteful ex-civil servant who snipes at the ideas of his time from a basement in St Petersburg. The Underground Man is bizarre, brilliant, tragic, unexpected – our scholars will tell us he's the first modern anti-hero, an early first-person voice, Dostoyevsky's first great work, the seed of later masterpieces. And all this is true, but here's the thing: within the concept of this disaffected man, and inside all his arguments, sits one stunning idea, one I feel is more relevant today than ever, one which not only made me sense a kindred spirit, but which licensed my humanity outright.

To even begin to introduce *Notes from Underground* I need to position air crashes and socks in your mind as extremes on the same spectrum. I'll sketch the spectrum like this: following the tragedy of September 2001, a decades-long inquiry was completed into human responses to mortal danger. Reports from the twin towers were combined with air-crash studies to show who we really are when the chips are down. And it turns out that eighty-five per cent of us, when faced with death unless we act, will do nothing. Others will panic uselessly. So that's extreme duress. At the other end of the spectrum – extreme absence of duress – is me finding socks. Which is to say, finding one, wandering around, leaving it behind, taking a shoe to find the other, returning with the sock but leaving the shoe behind. This is me, whose eyes only itch when there's something on my fingers which will hurt them. I don't say this is also you. But here's the point: there are enough of me around to ask which imbecile ever thought it a good idea to base social, political, and economic systems on the assumption that humans will act purposefully and correctly, even in their own best interests. Look around us, at economies, ideologies.

All have failed because their systems assume we will do the right thing.

This is the gift of *Notes from Underground*. Dostoyevsky dropped a pill into the middle of the nineteenth century and the thing is still fizzing: *existentialism*. The notion that history is not built from purposeful steps. That we might not be interested, obliged or even able to do the correct thing – that we might not know what the correct thing is, or care.

That basically we might not end up wanting to do *anything at all*.

Why did the teenager cross the road? Because somebody told him not to. This is the essence of the Underground Man, running the other way just to prove his autonomous

2

existence – except that in this case the philosophies grew far beyond the remit of a novel. They became ideas that continue to change the world. *Notes from Underground* first appeared in Russia in 1864, in the middle of one of history's most fertile periods. Of course the author was speaking to his time, addressing the discourses around him, as you'll see the Underground Man do in detail, but for me two things set the work apart from its time and pull it sharply into ours. The first is that Russian novels up to this point were concerned with action; they hung on what their characters did, while Dostoyevsky became concerned with motivation, with the curious machinations of the mind. He was a psychologist before psychology existed, and his observations were acute and universal. The second is the fact that the nineteenth-century themes addressed by the Underground Man are the seedlings of the themes of our day – industrialism, utopianism, western markets, the grip of science and technology on truth – and for me his arguments not only still apply but have new weight.

Still, all this thought is woven through the ramblings of an unpleasant and contradictory man, making it an artwork – the Underground Man spends the first section of this short novel in bitter monologue from his basement, and the second part narrating the scenes which led to his seclusion, and which may underpin his ideas. I say 'may' as he remains an unreliable narrator throughout. Only Dostoyevsky knew how much of the Underground Man was himself, but I can give you the clues I used to reconcile the author and his character.

I always felt a particular kinship with Dostoyevsky, perhaps from our having grown up in similar, walled compounds, having been warned not to explore outside alone, having ignored the warning and seen chaos, violence and cruelty first hand, and at a young age. Perhaps we were similarly addictive, rode similar roller coasters of fortune – we both took a kicking for second novels, both threw everything at our first. He even declared '*What matters is that my novel should cover everything. If it does not work I will hang myself.*'

Whereas I would have driven off a cliff.

It's easy to see historical figures as one-dimensional icons, their lives as full of aplomb as quotes by Oscar Wilde. But Fyodor Mikhailovich Dostoyevsky was not this way, and I realise the coincidences above are not the cause of my feeling; rather the feeling is one you and I both might have, in sharing his weaknesses. He was a sensitive man, as sensitive as a synapse, and deeply affected by life. He was insecure, by turns aloof or withdrawn, and one thing he almost certainly shared with the Underground Man was torment – while he wrote this book his wife lay dying, he was almost broke, having gambled his livelihood away, and his appeal as a writer was waning.

If this is your first Dostoyevsky, you've landed in a rich place. *Notes from Underground* sits bang in the middle of his output of major fiction. Moreover his story from this point has a happier ending, at least literarily, than the events above suggest. The books that followed include his masterpieces – the next work was *Crime and Punishment* – and all were coloured by the germ of this little book and its ideas.

Calculate the number of people across a century who were changed and inspired by Freud, Nietzsche, Sartre, Kafka, Orwell, and countless others – and know that they were changed and inspired by this book. It's a hell of a club to join, and this new translation by Natasha Randall erases a century of awkward word-for-word interpretations, which is like turning it from black-and-white back into colour; something

I feel has Dostoyevsky's own blessing, as a translator of literature himself.

There can't be a better moment for this book to find its way into your hands and your mind. I can only consign it to you with this advice:

Don't read it because it's great – read it because you don't have to.

DBC Pierre
October 2012

PART ONE

THE UNDERGROUND*

---

* Both the author of these notes and the 'notes' themselves, of course, are fictitious. Nonetheless, such personages as the writer of these notes not only may, but must exist in our society, if you take into consideration the general circumstances in which our society was formed. I wanted to bring before the face of the public, more evidently than usual, one of the characters of times recently passed. He is one of the representatives of a still-existing generation. In this fragment, entitled 'The Underground', this personage presents himself, his point of view, and he seems to want to clarify the reasons that caused his appearance and indeed forced his appearance in our midst. In the next fragment come the real 'notes' of this personage, about certain events of his life.

I

I am a sick person . . . A spiteful one. An unattractive person, too. I think my liver is diseased. But I don't give a damn about my disease and in fact I don't even know what's wrong with me. I do not seek treatment and have never sought treatment, though I respect medicine and doctors. Furthermore, I am superstitious to an extreme – well, only enough to respect medicine. (I am sufficiently educated that I shouldn't be superstitious, but I am superstitious.) No, sir, I won't seek treatment out of spite. And this, I suppose, you won't deign to understand. Well, sir, I do understand it. Of course, in this case, I won't be able to explain it to you, whom I season with my spite. I know perfectly well that I cannot 'befoul' the doctors with the fact that I'm not being treated by them; I know better than anyone that I am only harming myself with all this, and no one else. But nonetheless, if I do not seek treatment, it is out of spite. My little old liver is diseased – and may it be even more severely diseased!

I have been living like this for a while now – about twenty years. Now I'm forty. I used to be in the civil service, but now I'm not. I was a spiteful civil servant. I was rude and I found pleasure in it. I did not take bribes, you see, and consequently I had to reward myself with something. (A bad witticism, but I won't cross it out. I wrote it thinking that it would come out sharp-witted and now, as I can see for myself, I was just showing off grossly – I won't cross it out on purpose!) Whenever

9

people came to the desk where I sat, to ask for information, I'd gnash my teeth at them and I felt an inexorable pleasure when it succeeded in distressing someone. It almost always succeeded. For the most part they were a shy people; they were applicants, you know what I mean. Among the dandies, though, there was one officer in particular that I couldn't stand. He just wouldn't show any respect, and he clanked his sword in a loathsome way. I had a feud with him for a year and a half over that sword. I was victorious in the end. He stopped his clanking. But that happened in my youth.

Gentlemen, do you know what constituted the main point of my spitefulness? Well, there's the joke, there's the utter filthiness of it all – at every moment, even my most bilious moment, I could acknowledge to myself in shame that I am not a spiteful person, I'm not even an embittered one, I am only scaring sparrows in vain, and amusing myself with it. I may foam at the mouth, but bring me some kind of dolly to play with, give me a cup of tea with sugar, and I will likely settle down. My soul might soften, even, but no doubt afterwards I will probably gnash my teeth at you and then suffer from insomnia for several months out of shame. Such, indeed, is my habit.

I lied about myself just now, about being a spiteful civil servant. I lied with spite. I was just making mischief with the applicants and the officers, but in reality I could never be spiteful. At every moment I was conscious within myself of many, many elements most opposite to such spite. I felt that they were teeming within me, these contrary elements. I knew that they had been teeming within me my whole life and they had asked to be released but I wouldn't let them, I just wouldn't let them, I would not let them out on purpose. They tortured me to the point of shame; they led me to the point of convulsions – and I've had enough of them. I've really had enough! It must certainly seem to you, gentlemen, that I am now repenting of something before you, that I am asking that you forgive me for something. I am sure that it would seem so to you . . . However, I assure you, I don't care if it does indeed seem that way.

It wasn't just that I was unable to become spiteful, I couldn't become anything else either: I am not spiteful nor kind, not a scoundrel nor honest, not a hero nor an insect. Now, I am living out my days in my corner, teasing myself with the malicious, unhelpful consolation that an intelligent man cannot seriously make anything of himself, that only a fool can become something. Indeed, an intelligent man of the nineteenth century should be, and is morally obliged to be, for the most part, a characterless being; a man with character, a man of action is, for the most part, a limited being. This is my conviction of forty years. Now I am forty years old and yes, forty years is an entire lifetime; indeed it is deepest old age. It is unseemly to live beyond forty years – vulgar, immoral! Who lives beyond forty years – answer me in earnest, honestly? Well, I will tell you who does that: fools and rascals. I will say this to the face of all of my elders, to all those respectable elders, to all those silver-haired and sweet-smelling elders! I'll say it to the face of the whole world! I have the right to speak like this, since I myself will live to sixty years. To seventy years, I will live! To eighty years, I will live! Hold on! Let me catch my breath . . .

You probably think, gentlemen, that I want to make you laugh? Well, you're wrong about that, too. I am not as cheerful a man as it seems to you, or might seem to you; however, if you are irritated by all this chatter, (and I can already feel that you are irritated) then why not ask me, who am I? And to that I will answer: I am a collegiate assessor. I went into the civil service so I'd have something to eat (and only for this reason), and when last year one of my distant relatives left me six thousand roubles in his will, I immediately retired and settled into my own corner. I lived in this corner before but now I have settled into this corner. My room is rotten and awful, on the outskirts of the city. My maid is a village woman, old and lousy with stupidity, and moreover she always gives off a foul smell. They tell me that the Petersburg climate will be harmful for me and that with my paltry means it is very expensive to live in Petersburg. I know all this, more than those experienced and wise counsel-givers, and those that shake their heads. But I am staying in Petersburg; I will not leave Petersburg! I will not leave because . . . ah! Well, it doesn't matter at all, whether I leave or don't leave.

Now, what can a proper man speak about with utmost pleasure?

The answer: himself.

So then, I will talk about myself.

II

I would like now to tell you, gentlemen, whether or not you wish to hear it, why I have never been able to become even an insect. I will tell you solemnly that I have often wanted to become an insect. But I have yet to earn even that honour. I swear to you, gentlemen, that being too conscious is a disease, a real and total disease. Ordinary human consciousness would easily satisfy man's daily needs – that is, half or a quarter less than is apportioned to the developed man of the nineteenth century, who furthermore has the particular misfortune of living in St Petersburg, the most abstract and intentional city of the entire earthly sphere. (Cities occur as both intentional and unintentional.) It would have been completely sufficient, for example, to have the kind of consciousness with which all the so-called spontaneous people and men of action live. I'd place a bet that you think I'm writing this to show off, to be witty at the expense of men of action, and it's with bad taste that I show off, clanking my sword like that officer did. But, gentlemen, who can take pride in his diseases and then show off about them too?

But what am I on about – everyone does it; people take pride in their diseases, and I do perhaps more than anyone. Let's not argue; my objections were absurd. But all the same, I am firmly convinced that it is not just that a great deal of consciousness is a disease but that any kind of consciousness is a disease. I'll stand by that. But let's put that aside for a minute. Tell me something: why is it, as though on purpose, that at the exact, yes, at the very exact moments when I might be most conscious of the intricacies of 'all that is beautiful and elevated'[1] (as they used to say in these parts), it seems that I am not conscious of them, and I do such ugly deeds, which . . . well, yes, in short, everyone does, but which, to make things worse, occur to me just when I am most conscious of the fact that I should absolutely not do them? The more I was conscious of goodness and of all that is 'beautiful and elevated,' the deeper I sank into my mire and the more able I was to get completely stuck in it. But the main feature of all this was that it didn't seem to be accidental within me; it was as if it were meant to be so. It was as though this were my most normal condition and not at all a disease or corruption, so much so that finally the desire in me to struggle against this corruption passed. In the end, I nearly believed (or maybe I did believe in fact) that this, very likely, was indeed my normal condition. But to start with, at the beginning, how much torture did I endure in this struggle! I didn't believe that this happened to others, and so I hid this about myself my whole life, like a secret. I was ashamed (maybe I am ashamed even now); I went so far as to feel a little kind of mysterious, abnormal, base delight in frequently returning to my own corner, on particularly nasty Petersburg nights, and becoming increasingly conscious of the fact that I had done another mischief that day, and that what's done can't be undone, and that inwardly, secretly you gnaw and gnaw at yourself with your teeth, you nag at and suck yourself until the point when the bitter taste turns finally into a kind of ignominious, accursed sweetness and finally . . . into absolute, serious pleasure! Yes, into pleasure, into pleasure! I will stand by that. I have mentioned this as I want to know everything for certain: do others experience such pleasure? I will explain to you: this pleasure was derived precisely from an over-bright consciousness of my humiliation; from the fact that you already feel you've reached the final wall; that this is bad but that it can't be any other way; that there's no other way out for you, that you'll never make another person of yourself; that even if time and faith were sufficient for you to remake yourself into something else, then for sure, you wouldn't want to be remade anyway; but if you did want to, you'd still do nothing because in actuality, there might be nothing to remake yourself into. But mainly and ultimately, this all happens according to the normal and basic laws of heightened consciousness and from the inertia flowing straight from these laws, and consequently, it's not just that you won't remake yourself, you simply won't do anything at all. So one could conclude, for example, that the result of heightened consciousness is: yes, you're a scoundrel, and it's some kind of comfort to the scoundrel that he feels himself actually to be a scoundrel. But, enough. Ugh, I've talked a lot of nonsense, but what have I explained? How to explain this pleasure? Well, I'm explaining myself! I will take this to its conclusion! That is why I picked up my pen . . .

I, for example, am horribly proud. I'm as mistrustful and touchy as a hunchback or a dwarf, but it's true, I've experienced such moments that if someone had slapped me, I might even have been glad of it. I'm serious: I would probably have been able to discover in it my own kind of pleasure, the pleasure of despair, of course, but even in despair there are the most burning pleasures, especially when you are already very strongly conscious of the inevitability of your situation. And when you are slapped, you are struck with the consciousness of the grease you've been rubbed with. The main thing is that no matter how you pitch it, it comes out that I am always the most to blame, and most insulting of all is that I'm to blame without blame, so to speak, according to the laws of nature. I am to blame as I am cleverer than those around me. (I always consider myself to be cleverer than those around me, and sometimes, would you believe, I have even been ashamed of it. At least, throughout my life I have always looked away and have never been able to look people right in the eye.)

But in the end I am to blame because, even if I had possessed magnanimity, then I would have more suffering from the consciousness of its total uselessness. Indeed, I could probably do nothing with my magnanimity: I couldn't forgive, because the offender, possibly, hit me according to the laws of nature, and you can't forgive the laws of nature; nor could

I forget, because though they are the laws of nature, it's insulting all the same. Finally, even if I'd wanted to be totally magnanimous and to the contrary had desired to take revenge on my insulter, then I wouldn't be able to get revenge on anyone because it is certain that I wouldn't have had the resolve to do anything even if I could have. And why wouldn't I have had the resolve? About this I want to say a couple of words especially.

III

For those people who are able to take revenge on others and generally stand up for themselves – how does it come to pass, for example? It seizes them, let's say, this feeling of vengeance, and then nothing else remains in their being apart from this feeling. Such a gentleman just barges straight towards his goal, like a maddened bull dipping its horns, and nothing but a wall will stop him. (Incidentally, in the face of a wall, such gentlemen, that is spontaneous people and men of action, sincerely give up. The wall is not an obstacle for them as it is for us thinking and therefore not active people; it isn't a pretext to turn off the path, a pretext in which our brotherhood usually doesn't believe but which we are always glad to follow. No, they give up in all sincerity. The wall, to them, has something of a calming effect, it is morally settling and conclusive, perhaps even mystical . . . but more later on the wall.)

So, I consider such a spontaneous man to be a real, normal man, just as tender Mother Nature wanted to see him when she graciously delivered him to this earth. I envy such a man to a bilious extreme. He is stupid, I'm not arguing with you on that, but maybe the normal man should be stupid – how do we know? Maybe this is a very beautiful fact, even. And I am furthermore convinced of the suspicion, so to speak, that if you take the antithesis of a normal man, that's to say a man of heightened consciousness, who comes not from the bosom of nature, of course, but from a distilling jar (this is almost mysticism at this point, gentlemen, and I am suspicious of that, also), then this distilling-jar man sometimes gives up in the face of his antithesis, so that, with all his heightened consciousness, in good conscience, he considers himself to be a mouse, and not a man. He may well be a mouse of heightened consciousness, but he's a mouse all the same, and here's this man before him, and so, therefore . . . and so on. And, most importantly, he thinks himself a mouse; no one asks this of him, and this is an important point.

Let's now look at this mouse in action. Suppose, for example, that it has also been insulted (and it is almost always insulted) and it also wants to get revenge. Perhaps even more spite will have accumulated in it than in *l'homme de la nature et de la verité*. The vile and base desire to repay the offender with the same malice may scratch even more nastily within it than in *l'homme de la nature et de la verité*, because *l'homme de la nature et de la verité*, according to his inborn stupidity, considers his revenge to be justice, plain and simple; but the mouse, as a result of his heightened consciousness, says there is no justice here. We come, eventually, to the matter itself, to the act of vengeance itself. The unfortunate mouse, apart from one initial mischief, has managed already to heap up around himself, in the guise of questions and doubts, a great deal of other mischiefs. This single question has brought up so many unresolved questions, that against its will some accursed muck has collected around it, a stinking filth, made up of its doubts, worries and finally, of spittle, pouring forth upon it from the spontaneous men of action, solemnly surrounding it as judges and dictators, laughing at it with the full force of their hearty throats. Of course, all that it can do then is wave it all away with its paw and, with a smile of assumed contempt, which it doesn't itself believe, crawl shamefully into its mouse hole. There, in the vile and stinking underground, our insulted, downtrodden, ridiculed mouse is immediately buried in a cold, venomous and above all, everlasting spite. For forty years running it will remember its insult to the last, most shameful, detail and each time it will add even more shameful details of its own, spitefully teasing and irritating itself with its own fantasies. It will be ashamed itself of its fantasies, but nonetheless it will remember everything, twist everything, inventing fables about itself, under the pretext that they also might well have happened, and it won't forgive anything. Perhaps it will start to get its revenge somehow, in fits and starts, in trifles, from behind the stove, incognito, not believing in either its right to get revenge nor in the success of its revenge, and knowing in advance that with all its attempts to get revenge, it will suffer itself a hundred times more than him on whom it seeks revenge, and that person, probably, won't even feel an itch. On its deathbed it will again remember everything, with an interest that has amassed during all that time and . . . But it is exactly in this, the cold, foul half-despair, half-belief; in this conscious burying of oneself alive in the underground for forty years out of woe; in the strongly founded and yet somewhat doubtful hopelessness of its situation; in all the venom of unsatisfied desire that has entered inside; in this fever of vacillations, the decisions that took forever and then in one minute were taken with regret . . . in all this can be found the essence of that strange pleasure about which I was speaking. It is so subtle, so unyielding to consciousness sometimes, that even slightly limited people or simply people with strong nerves won't understand a single feature of it.

'Maybe some others won't understand it either,' you add, grinning, 'like those who have never had a slap in the face.' And you will be hinting at me that perhaps I have also experienced in my life a slap in the face and that's why I speak like an expert. I'd wager that you think that. But calm down, gentlemen, I haven't received a slap in the face, even though it would be all the same to me, no matter what you may think of it. Maybe I myself regret that I haven't been slapped in the face too often in my life. But that's enough, not one more word on this subject that is so extraordinarily interesting to you.

I will calmly continue describing people with strong nerves who don't understand this particular refinement of pleasure. These gentlemen, in certain cases, for example, may bellow like bulls with the full force of their voices and even though, let's say, this brings them great honour, in the face of the impossible, as I have already explained, they submit themselves at once. The impossible – meaning the stone wall? Which stone wall? Well, of course, the laws of nature, the conclusions of the natural sciences and mathematics. As soon as they prove to you, for example, that you are descended from the monkey, then there's no point in grimacing, just take it for what it is. As soon as they prove to you that in actuality, one drop of your own fat should be more valuable to you than a hundred thousand of your brethren, and this conclusion finally settles all the so-called virtues and duties and other ravings and prejudices, then take it as such; there's nothing else to do because two times two is mathematics. Just you try and refute it. 'For goodness' sake,' they'll shout at you, 'you musn't protest: two twos are four! Nature isn't asking your permission, her business is nothing to do with your desires and whether you like her laws or you don't. You are obliged to accept her just as she is, and consequently, all her conclusions as well. A wall, therefore, is a wall . . . etc., etc.'

Good God, what are the laws of nature and arithmetic to me, when for some reason I don't like these laws and the idea that two times two is four? Clearly, I won't break through that wall with my forehead if indeed I don't have the strength to break through it, but I won't be reconciled with it only because I have a stone wall before me and I lack the strength.

It's as though such a stone wall is in fact a reassurance and does in fact contain some signal to the world, simply because it is two-times-two-is-four. Oh, the absurdity of absurdities! But it is quite a different matter to understand everything, to be aware of everything, all impossibilities and the stone wall; or to be reconciled with none of these impossibilities and stone walls, if it disgusts you to be so reconciled; or to follow the path of the most inevitable, logical combinations to the most revolting conclusion on the eternal theme that says that you may find yourself to blame for something even in a stone wall, even though it is starkly evident that you're not to blame at all, and consequently, powerlessly and silently, you gnash your teeth, sensually frozen into inertia, dreaming about the fact that it turns out that there's no one to spite; that you won't find an object for it, and maybe you will never find one, that this is a swindle, a fiddling, a card-sharping, that this is just gruel; no one knows who and no one knows what, but despite all these unknowns and fiddlings it still hurts you and the more unknown to you, the more it hurts!

IV

'Ha, ha, ha! And now you'll say that you derive pleasure in your toothache!' you gentlemen will cry out, laughing.

'And what of it? There is pleasure even in a toothache,' I reply. My teeth once hurt for a whole month so I know there is. Then, of course, you aren't just angry in silence but with groans; but these groans are not earnest, these are malicious groans, and in this malice is the whole joke. It is with these groans that the pleasure of the sufferer is expressed; if he didn't feel pleasure in them, he wouldn't start groaning. This is a good example, gentlemen, and I will develop it. These groans express, firstly, a consciousness in us of the whole humiliating pointless-ness of your pain; the whole of natural law, which you spit upon, of course, but from which you suffer all the same, while she does not. They (the groans) express the consciousness that you won't find an enemy but that the pain is real; the conscious-ness that you, despite all possible Wagenheims,[2] are in total slavery to your teeth; that if someone so wishes, your teeth will stop hurting and if they don't wish it then you'll be in pain for another three months; and that, finally, if you are still being contrary and are protesting all the same, then all that is left to you for your own consolation is to flog yourself or to punch the wall as painfully as you can, and decidedly nothing more. Well, it is with these bloody insults, this mockery from an unknown person, that the pleasure finally starts and then gives way sometimes to the highest sensuality. I beg you, gentlemen, to listen some time to the groans of an educated man of the nineteenth century who is suffering with a toothache. On about the second or third day of his illness he starts already not to groan like he did on the first day, that's to say, not just from the aching of his teeth, not like some kind of coarse *muzhik*,[3] but like a person touched by progress and European civilisation, like a person who has 'renounced his soil and folk origins,' as the expression goes these days. His groans become sort of nastily vicious, and they continue for whole days and nights. And he knows himself that these groans are of no help to him; he knows better than anyone that he is only futilely straining and irritating himself and others; he knows that even the audience for whom he is exerting himself, together with his whole household, are already listening to him with loathing, they don't believe him for even a half-*kopeck* piece, and they know that he could groan in a different way, more simply, without the roulades and the capers, and that he is only doing so out of malice, fooling around out of malice. And so there it is, the sensuality lies in such consciousness and disgrace. He's saying 'I am disturbing you, I am straining your hearts, I am not letting anyone sleep. Well then, don't sleep, feel it yourself, every minute of my toothache. I am not a hero to you now, as I wanted earlier to seem, but just a bit of a nasty person, a *chenapan*.[4] So be it! I am very glad that you have sussed me out. Is it awful for you to listen to my despicable little groans? Well, let it be awful. Now I'll give you an even more awful roulade . . .' Don't you understand now, gentlemen? No, it's clear, one must cultivate and expand one's consciousness to the extreme in order to understand all the intricacies of this sensuality! You laugh? Very pleased. My jokes, gentlemen, are in bad taste, of course, they're uneven, contra-dictory and lacking self-confidence. But this is because I do not respect myself. Can a conscious man respect himself to any degree?

V

Now, can it be possible, can it really be possible for a man to respect himself in any measure when he derives pleasure from the very feeling of his humiliation? I am not now speaking from some sickly sweet remorse. No, I was never able to bear saying 'Forgive me, Papa, I won't do it again.' Not because I wasn't capable of saying it, but the opposite – maybe it was exactly because I happened to be too capable of it, much too much! As though I used to trip into such situations where I wasn't to blame, not even in spirit or fantasy, on purpose. That was the foulest part of it all. At such times I would become tenderhearted, repent, pour tears forth, and of course I'd tricked myself into it and wasn't pretending at all. My heart had already somehow turned foul. And not even the laws of nature could be blamed at this point, though the laws of nature have offended me continuously and more than anything in my life. It's awful to remember it all, indeed it was awful at the time. A minute or so later I would realise with spite that it was all a lie, a lie, a disgusting affected lie, that's to say all the remorse, all the tenderheartedness, all the vows of renewal. But you ask why did I misspeak and torture myself like this? The answer: because it was boring to sit with my arms folded so I took to various antics. That's right. Observe yourselves better, gentlemen, and then you will see that I'm right. I thought up adventures and invented a life in order to live a little. How many times has it happened that, say, I simply took offence, for no reason, on purpose; and of course one knows one is not offended by anything, that one is putting it on, but one arrives at such a point that in the end one has actually taken offence in earnest. My whole life I've tended to play such games, so that in the end I'd lost all power over myself. Another time, twice even, I tried to force myself to fall in love. I suffered indeed, gentlemen, I assure you. My suffering isn't really believable in the depths of my soul since there's a certain mockery stirring there, but I did suffer, even in a real and honest-to-god way; I'd get jealous, leave my senses . . . And all out of ennui, gentlemen, all out of ennui; inertia descends on me. The direct, legitimate, immediate fruit of consciousness is inertia, that is conscious folded-arm-sitting. I have already referred to this above. I repeat, emphatically repeat: all spontaneous people and men of action are active exactly because they are dim and limited. How can I explain? Here's how: as a result of their limitations they take the nearest and secondary causes for primary ones, and in this way they are more quickly and easily persuaded than other people that they have found the indisputable basis for their action, and that eases their minds; and that's the most important thing. Yes, to begin an action one must be totally becalmed before-hand and all doubts must have been banished. So how do I, for example, becalm myself? Where are the primary causes that I can lean on, what foundations do I have? Where am I to get them? I make exercises in thinking, and therefore every primary cause immediately drags after itself another, even more primary cause and so on, in perpetuity. Such is the essence of all consciousness and thought. So again, these are the laws of nature. And what in the end is the result? Always the same. Remember, I was speaking about revenge just now. (You probably didn't take it in.) What was said: a man takes revenge because he finds justice in it. Which means he has found a primary cause, found a basis and that is: justice. So he is calmed on all sides and therefore takes his revenge calmly and successfully, as though he's convinced he has done an honest and just deed. But I see no justice here, and I don't find any virtue either and therefore, if I'm about to take revenge then it's only out of spite. Spite, of course, can displace everything, all my doubts, and so it can serve very effectively as a primary cause exactly because it isn't a cause at all. But what can I do if I lack spite? (I'm back where I started just now). My spite, again a result of these accursed laws of consciousness, chemically disintegrates. You look at it and the object takes flight, the reasons evaporate, the culprit can't be found, the offence becomes not an offence but a *fatum*, something like a toothache for which no one is to blame, and therefore, what's left is the very same answer, which is to beat the wall even more painfully. So you dismiss it with a wave of hand because you haven't found the primary cause. But just try to get carried away blindly by your feelings, without reasoning, without a primary cause, chasing off consciousness at least for the time being; hate a bit or love a little, only so you won't sit with folded arms. The day after tomorrow, at the very latest, you will start to loathe yourself for the fact that you fooled yourself knowingly. The result: a soap bubble and inertia. Oh, gentlemen, it might just be that I consider myself to be an intelligent man because I have never managed to start or finish anything in my whole life. Yes, yes I'm a chatterbox, a harmless, annoying chatterbox, like we all are. But what is to be done if the direct and only task of every intelligent man is to chatter, that is, an intentional pouring from the empty to the emptier.

VI

Oh, if only it was just from laziness that I do nothing. Lord, how I could respect myself then. I could respect myself exactly because I was at least in the right condition to have laziness within me; there would be at least one characteristic, a positive one so to speak, of which I could be confident. The question: who is this? The answer: an idler. Now that would be something very pleasant to hear about oneself. It means I would be positively defined, it means there was something to be said about me. 'Idler!' Indeed, this is a title and an appointment, it's a career, good sir. Don't mock it, it's true. I would then be a member by rights of the very best club itself and would be busy respecting myself without pause. I knew a gentleman who was proud his whole life of the fact that he knew what he was talking about when it came to Château Lafite. He considered it to be his most positive quality and never doubted himself. He died, not only with a peaceful conscience but with a triumphant one, and he was quite right. I should have chosen a career: I would be an idler and a glutton, and not a simple one but, say, one who was sympathetic to all that is 'beautiful and elevated'. How do you like that? I have long imagined it. This 'beautiful and elevated' has weighed heavily on my head these forty years. Those were my forty years – but it would have, oh it would have been different! I would have sought for myself a corresponding activity, namely drinking to all that was beautiful and elevated. I would seize every opportunity to first shed a tear into my glass and then to drink it in the name of all that is beautiful and elevated. I would then turn everything in this world into the beautiful and the elevated; I would have found all that was beautiful and elevated in the most vile, unquestionable rubbish. I would be as given to crying as a wet sponge. An artist, for example, has painted a Ge picture.[5] I would immediately drink to the health of the artist who painted this Ge picture because I love all that is beautiful and elevated. A writer has written *Whomever It Pleases*;[6] I'll drink straight away to the health of *Whomever It Pleases* because I love all that is beautiful and elevated. I would demand respect for this, and I would persecute anyone who didn't show me respect. I would live peacefully, die triumphantly – what a delight, a total delight! And what a paunch I will have grown myself, what a triple chin I will have erected, what a ruby nose I will have manufactured, so that every person I encounter would say upon looking at me, 'Here is a plus sign! Now here's a real positive!' And say what you like, it is very pleasant to hear such testimonials in our negative age, gentlemen.

VII

But these are all golden dreams. Oh, tell me, who was it that first announced, that first proclaimed that man only does mischiefs because he doesn't know his real interests; and that if you were to enlighten him, to open his eyes to his real, normal interests, then a man would immediately stop doing mischiefs and become kind and noble, because being enlightened and understanding his real advantages he would see advantage for himself in goodness, and everyone knows that no man can act knowingly against his own advantages. Therefore, so to speak, would he begin to do good out of necessity? Oh, the infant! Oh, the pure, innocent child! When, first of all, in all these thousands of years, has man acted only for his own advantage? What is to be done with the millions of facts that witness that people *well within their ken*, that is in full understanding of their real advantages, have left these advantages in the background and have thrown themselves down another path, toward risk, toward chance, not impelled by anyone or anything but as though it is simply that they do not want to follow the indicated path, and being stubborn, willful, they strike out onto another, hard-going, absurd path, seeking it out just before darkness falls. So, that means that this stubbornness and willfullness were actually more pleasant to them than any advantage. Advantage! What is an advantage? And will you take it upon yourself to define in what, specifically, man's advantage consists? And what if it happens that a man's advantage *sometimes* doesn't just possibly but necessarily consist of man's desire to do what is bad for him and not what is advantageous? And if that is so, if such a situation is possible, then the whole theory turns to dust. What do you think – do such situations occur? You laugh. Well, laugh then, gentlemen, but just answer this: is it possible to assess reliably man's advantages? Aren't there some that not only have not been included but that are somehow impossible to classify? You, gentlemen, as far as I know, have taken your whole register of man's advantages from the averages of statistical figures and scientific-economic formulae. Indeed, your advantages are prosperity, wealth, liberty, peace and so on and so on. And therefore the man who would blatantly and knowingly go against that entire register would be, to your mind, and yes of course to mine, an obscurantist or perfectly insane, right? But then here is what is surprising: how does it happen that all of these statisticians, wise men and lovers of humankind, when considering man's advantages persistently leave one advantage out? They don't even take it into consideration in the way they should, and the whole of their consideration depends on it. It wouldn't be a big deal to take it, this advantage, and to put it on the list. But that's the trouble, that this strange advantage doesn't fall into any category, has no place on any list. I have a friend, for example . . . Eh, gentlemen! He is your friend too; and for whom – for whom! – isn't he a friend? In preparing for an activity, this gentleman will immediately lay out for you, eloquently and clearly, how exactly he must act according to the laws of reason and truth. Moreover, he will speak to you with excitement and passion about real, normal human interests; with mockery he will reproach short-sighted fools who understand neither their own advantages nor the real meaning of virtue; and exactly a quarter of an hour later, not for any accidental, external reason but from something particularly internal which is stronger than all of his interests, he throws out his other knee altogether,[7] that is, he will blatantly go off against that which he has just been saying: against the laws of reason, and against his own advantage, and well, in a word, against everything. I warn you that my friend is a compound person, and so it is hard somehow to blame him. That's just the thing, gentlemen, there seems to exist something that is dearer to any man than the very best of advantages, or let's say (not to violate reason) that there is one, most advantageous advantage (specifically, the missing one we were just talking about) which is more important and more advantageous than all the other advantages and for which a man, if necessary, is prepared to go against all rules, that is against reason, honour, peace, prosperity – essentially, against all these splendid and useful things, if only to attain this primary, most advantageous advantage, which is dearest of all to him.

'But it's an advantage nonetheless,' you will say, interrupting me. Sir, we will clarify the matter, this isn't just a play on words, but the point is that this advantage is remarkable for the very reason that it destroys all our classifications and consistently shatters all the systems that were established by the lovers of humankind for the happiness of humankind. In a word, it disturbs everything. But before I name this advantage for you, I want to compromise myself personally and so I boldly proclaim that all these splendid systems, all these theories that may clarify to humankind their real and normal interests so that they necessarily strive to achieve these interests and in doing so become kind and noble, are thus far, in my opinion, merely logistics! Yes, sirs, logistics! Indeed, to maintain this theory that one can rehabilitate humankind by means of a system of his advantages, well, this, in my opinion, is almost the same as . . . well, maintaining, for example, as Buckle did, that humankind softens with civilisation and therefore becomes less bloodthirsty and less capable of war. This is what he concludes, it seems, according to logic. But a man is so prone to systems and to abstract conclusions that he is prepared to distort the truth on purpose, prepared to deny the visible and the audible just so he can justify his own logic. I use this example because it is an exceedingly bright one. Just look around yourself: rivers of blood flood along, in the cheeriest of ways, just like champagne. Take the whole of our nineteenth century, in which Buckle lived, too. Take Napoleon, both the great one and the present one. Take North America, the eternal union. Take, finally, the caricature of Schleswig-Holstein. And what exactly does civilisation soften in us? Civilisation just produces many facets of sensation in a person and . . . absolutely nothing more. And through the development of these many facets, a person may perhaps come to the point of finding pleasure in blood. Indeed, this has already happened. Have you noticed that the most refined blood-spillers are almost all the most civilised gentlemen, and all the various Attilas and Stenka Razins[8] wouldn't even be suitable as boot soles for them,[9] and even if they don't strike your eye as brightly as Attila and Stenka Razin, it's exactly because you come across them too often, they are too normal, they've become familiar. Man has become if not more blood-thirsty from civilisation then at least worse probably, and more vile in his bloodthirstiness than before. Before, he saw justice in bloodshed, and exterminated whomever he must with a calm conscience; now, we consider bloodshed to be a nasti-ness, and nonetheless we engage in this nastiness, and even more than previously. What's worse? Decide for yourselves. They say that Cleopatra (excuse me for the example from Roman history) loved to stick gold pins into the breasts of her slave-girls and derived pleasure from their screams and writhing. You will say that those were times, in comparative terms, of barbarism; and that these are also times of barbarism because (also in comparative terms) people still get stuck with pins; now, too, even though a person has learned to see things more clearly than in times of barbarism, he is still far from *learning* how to behave as his reason and the sciences would direct him. But all the same, you are perfectly sure that he cannot fail to understand once certain old bad habits have passed and once common sense and science will have totally re-educated and properly aligned human nature. You are sure that at that point man will himself cease to make mistakes voluntarily and, so to speak, will want, against his will, to link his will to his normal interests. Moreover, then, you say, science itself will teach man (but that is already a luxury, I think), that really he had neither will nor caprice, and never did, and that he himself is nothing more than something like a piano key or an organ stop; and that above all, there are laws of nature in the world; and so everything that he does is done not according to his wants but according to the laws of nature in and of themselves. Therefore these laws of nature need only be discovered and man will no longer have to answer for his behaviour and living will become extraordinarily easy. All human behaviour, it goes without saying, will be counted then according to these laws, mathematically, in something like logarithmic tables up to 108,000 and entered into the calendar; or even better than that, various well-intentioned publications will appear, like today's encyclo-paedic lexicons, in which everything will be so exactly calculated and explained that there won't be any more initi-atives or adventures in the world. 'And then,' this is you speaking still, 'new economic relationships will be established, completely prepared in advance and calculated with mathe-matical exactitude, so that in one instant every possible ques-tion will disappear, essentially because every possible answer will be provided.' Then the crystal palace will be built. Then . . . Well, in a word, the bird Kagan will land.[10] Of course, it can't be guaranteed (this is still you speaking), that then it won't be, for example, horribly boring (because what is there to do when all is formulated into a table), but then again, everything will be extraordinarily prudent. Of course, one might think up all manner of things from boredom! And it is also from boredom that gold pins get stuck into people, but that wouldn't matter.' What is bad (this is me speaking again) is that gold pins would perhaps then be something good, worth celebrating. Man is stupid indeed, phenomenally stupid. That is, he is not stupid at all but he is so ungrateful that you won't find another like him. I, for example, would not be in the least surprised if suddenly out of thin air, in the midst of this general future prudence, there arose some gentleman with an ignoble, or better, with a retrograde and mocking physiognomy, throwing open his arms and saying to us all, 'Come, gentlemen, let's give all this prudence a good kick, turn it to dust, with the sole purpose of sending all these logarithms to the devil so that we may be once again able to live according to our own stupid will!' That wouldn't matter either but what is annoying is that he would inevitably find followers: that is how man is tempered. And this is all for the very emptiest of reasons, about which it seems it isn't even worth thinking: it is precisely because man, always and everywhere, whoever he may be, has loved to act just as he pleases, and not at all as his reason and advantage would dictate; one can have a desire that is also against one's own advantage, and sometimes one *positively must* (this is my idea). One's own voluntary and free desire, one's own caprices, as wild as they are, one's fantasy, excited sometimes to the point of madness – this, all this is exactly that overlooked most advantageous of advantages, which doesn't fall into any classification and from which all systems and theories are permanently sent to hell. And what seized all those wise men and had them thinking that man must want some kind of normal, some kind of virtuous desire? Man wants *independent* desire alone, no matter what this independence costs and no matter where it may lead him. But this desire, the devil knows . . .

VIII

'Ha! ha! ha! But in reality there's no such thing as desire, if you please!' You will interrupt me with your laughing. 'Science has by now succeeded in anatomising man to such an extent that it is understood that desire and so-called free will is nothing other than . . .'

Hold on, gentlemen, I wanted to begin with that myself. I confess, I was frightened. I was just wanting to shout out that the devil only knows what desire comes from, and perhaps we ought to thank God for that, and then I remembered about science . . . and I took a step back. And then you started talking about it. Indeed, if in fact one day they find some kind of formula for all our desires and caprices, that is, what they depend upon, from which laws they have emerged, how exactly they have been disseminated, where they are directed in such and such situations and so on and so on – a real mathematical formula, that is – then man will immediately, perhaps, stop his desiring, and not just perhaps but for certain. What kind of wanting can it be when it is wanted according to a table? Moreover, he will turn immediately from a man into an organ stop or something similar; because what is a man without his passion, without will and without desire, if not a stop in an organ pipe? What do you think? Let us work out the probability – is this possible, or not?

'Hm,' you consider, 'our desires are for the most part mistaken due to a mistaken view of our advantages. That is why we sometimes want pure rubbish, because in our folly, through this rubbish, we see the easiest path to gaining some presumed advantage. And, well, when all this will be talked through and accounted for on paper (which is very possible, because it is vile and senseless to believe that there are some laws of nature that man will never understand), then, it stands to reason, there won't be so-called desires. Indeed, if desire should absolutely align with reason at some point then we will reason and not want, essentially because it will be impossible, really, for example, in preserving reason, to *want* the nonsensical and therefore knowingly to go against reason and to want to do ourselves harm. And since all desire and reason can be calculated, because at some point they will discover laws for our so-called free will, then, therefore, and this isn't a joke, it will be possible to make up some kind of table, so that we will actually want according to this table. Indeed, for example, if at some time, it can be proved to me that if I bite my thumb at someone then it is precisely because I am not able not to do it, and that I was certain to do it with that particular finger – so then what of *freedom* is left to me, especially if I am educated and have taken a course of science somewhere? Well, then I can calculate the next thirty years of my life. Basically, if it can be structured thus then there's nothing more for us to do; we'll have to accept it. And we should, in general, tirelessly repeat to ourselves that inevitably, at a certain moment and under certain circumstances, nature doesn't ask our permission; that we have to take her just as she is and not as we imagine her to be, and if we really aspire to tables and calendars, and, um . . . and even the distilling jar, then what can be done, we'll have to accept the distilling jar as it is, too! Or it will be accepted anyway, never mind you.'

Yes, sirs, now here I come to a dead end! Gentlemen, please excuse me that I have been over-philosophising; I've been underground for forty years! Allow me to fantasise a little. Do you see? Reason, gentlemen, is a good thing, that's indisputable, but reason is only reason and satisfies only the rational abilities of a man, whereas desire is a manifestation of one's whole life, that is, all of human life, including reason and including all its little itches. And although, due to this manifestation, our life often turns out to be rubbish, it is a life all the same, and not just the extraction of square roots. Indeed, for example, I, as is perfectly natural, want to live in order to satisfy my capacity for living, and not in order to satisfy my rational abilities alone, that is some twentieth part of my capacity for life. What does reason know? Reason knows only that which it has succeeded in learning (some things, perhaps it will never know; though this is not a comfort, but why not express it anyway?) and human nature acts as a whole, with everything that is in it, consciously and unconsciously, and though it may deceive, it lives nonetheless. I suspect, gentlemen, that you look upon me with pity; you will repeat to me that an enlightened and developed man cannot, in essence, no matter what future man is like, he cannot know-ingly want something for himself that is unadvantageous, and that this is mathematics. I agree with you totally, it is indeed mathematics. But I will repeat to you for the hundredth time, that there is just one situation, just one, when a man might purposefully, consciously desire something which is harmful to him and which is foolish, the most foolish thing of all, even. Specifically: *to have the right* to want something for himself which is most foolish and not to be bound by the obligation of desiring only intelligent things for himself. This most foolish thing, this caprice of ours, might actually be, gentlemen, more advantageous than anything else in the world, especially in certain situations. And in particular, it may be more advantageous than any advantage, even in those situations when it brings us obvious harm and contradicts the most sound conclusions of our reason on the subject of advantage, because in any case it preserves for us what is most important, most dear, and that is our personality, our individuality. Some claim that this is actually the most dear thing to a man; and desire, of course, if he wants it to, can coincide with reason, especially if it is not abused but used moderately; this is both useful and even sometimes praiseworthy. But desire very often, indeed most of the time, completely and stubbornly contradicts reason and . . . and . . . did you know that this is also useful and even sometimes very praiseworthy? Gentlemen, let's suppose that man is not stupid. (Really, this musn't at all be said about him, if only for the reason that if he is stupid, who then is intelligent?) But if he isn't stupid then he is nonetheless monstrously ungrateful! Phenomenally ungrateful. I even think that the best definition of man is this: a being on two legs that is ungrateful. But that's not all; this is not even his major deficiency; his most major deficiency is his perpetual misbehaviour; it is continuous, starting with the worldwide flood, right up to the Schleswig-Holstein period of man's fate.[11] It is misbehaviour and therefore also imprudence; for it has long been known that imprudence comes from nothing other than misbehaviour. Try casting a glance back at the history of mankind and what will you see? Is it majestic? Call it majestic if it pleases you. The Colossus of Rhodes is, for one thing, worth something! It was not for nothing that Mr Anaevsky[12] testified that some say it was the work of man's

FYODOR DOSTOYEVSKY

hand and others insist that it was created by nature herself.
Is it colourful? Perhaps it is colourful; you need only to look
through the full dress uniforms, military and civilian, of all
nations and all eras – that alone is worth something – and
then take the uniforms of the lower ranks and you could
really trip over: not one historian would remain standing.
Monotonous? Yes, monotonous if you like: they fight and they
fight, and they fight now and fought before and they fought
again after that – you will agree that this is just too monotonous. In a word, you can say anything about world history,
anything that might enter the head of the most disordered
imagination. There's one thing you can't say, though – that
it shows prudence. The first word would stick in your throat.
And here's the sort of thing that you'll encounter at every
turn: such moral and prudent people are constantly turning
up in life, such wise men and lovers of humankind who give
themselves the lifelong goal of conduct as moral and prudent
as possible, who, so to speak, illuminate themselves amongst
others specifically in order to prove that it is actually possible
to live one's life on this earth morally and prudently. What
next? It is common knowledge that many of these lovers
sooner or later, toward the end of their lives, cheat on themselves, producing some anecdote, sometimes even a most
indecent one. Now I ask you: what can you expect of a man
as a being on whom is bestowed such strange qualities? Shower
him with all earthly blessings, drown him in happiness totally
up to his head, so much so that only little bubbles leap up to
the surface of this happiness, as they do on water; give him
such economical satisfaction that he would have nothing at
all more to do than to sleep, to eat gingerbread and to trouble
himself over the ceaselessness of world history – and then,
right there, this man, from ingratitude alone, from calumny

38

alone, will do something nasty. He will even risk his ginger-bread and will purposely want the most pernicious rubbish, the most uneconomical nonsense, solely in order to mix into all this positive prudence his own pernicious fantastical element. It is exactly this, his fantastic dreams, his most vulgar stupidity, that he will want to hold close to himself for the sole purpose of confirming to himself (as if it were really necessary), that people are still people and not piano keys upon which the laws of nature play with their own hands, threatening to play them so much that it will be impossible to want anything that is not according to the calendar. And then, moreover, even if it is the case that he really does turn out to be a piano key, and if this was proven to him with natural sciences and mathematics, he would not see reason there and then but would do the opposite on purpose, solely out of ingratitude; essentially in order to stand his ground. And if the means don't present themselves, in that case he will think up destruction and chaos, he will think up different sufferings and will insist on standing his ground! He will unleash curses on the world, and since only man can deliver curses (this is his privilege, the main thing that differentiates him from other animals), then perhaps with this curse he will attain his purpose, that is to really convince himself that he is a man and not a piano key! If you say that all this can be calculated using a table, including chaos and darkness and curses, then the mere possibility of a prior calculation could stop it all and reason would take its hold. In such a case man would make himself crazy on purpose, so that he wouldn't have reason and could stand his ground! I believe in this, I answer for it, because the whole of man's work seems to consist of nothing else but the constant proving to himself that he is a man and not a piano key! It may cost him his skin, he may have to prove it by becoming a savage. And such being the case, how can one resist the urge to rejoice that this hasn't yet come to pass, and that desire still depends on something unknown to us?

You will shout at me (that is, if you deign to do so) that no one is confiscating my free will, that they're only meddling so that somehow it can be arranged that my free will, of its free will, would fall into line with my own normal interests, with the laws of nature and arithmetic.

Oh, gentlemen, what kind of personal free will can remain when the matter is driven to tabulation and arithmetics, when only two-times-two-is-four is the trend? Two times two will be four, regardless of my will. Such is free will for you!

IX

Gentlemen, I am joking of course, and I know it myself that I'm not joking successfully, but you can't take everything as a joke, after all. Maybe I am joking while gnashing my teeth. Gentlemen, questions torment me; resolve them for me. You, for example, want to rid man of his old habits and to correct his will in accordance with the demands of science and common sense. But how do you know that it is not only possible but it is also *necessary* to remake man in such a way? And why do you conclude that man's desire is so absolutely *necessary* to correct? In a word, how do you know that such a correction will really bring advantage to man? And, if we're going this far then why are you so *certainly* convinced that it is always advantageous to mankind, and that it is indeed a law for all of mankind that man not contradict his real, normal interests which are guaranteed by the conclusions of reason and arithmetic? So far, this is still only a supposition on your part. Let's suppose it's a law of logic, and not of mankind at all. Gentlemen, do you, perhaps, think that I am mad? Allow me to speak for myself. I agree: man is an animal, for the most part a creative one, prone to striving for a goal consciously and to engaging in the arts of engineering, that is, always and constantly forging new paths *wherever they may lead*. But the reason, maybe, that he wants sometimes to go off on a tangent is because he is *predestined* to forge this path, and perhaps also because however stupid the spontaneous man of action is in general, all the same the thought will sometimes occur to him that this path will almost always lead *somewhere or other*, and that the main thing is not where it leads but rather that it just goes somewhere, and that the well-behaved child, even in defiance of the engineering arts, does not succumb to a fatal laziness, which we all know to be the mother of all vices. Man likes to create and lay down paths, that is indisputable. But why does he also love destruction and chaos so passionately? Tell me that! And about that I would like to say a couple of words in particular. Might it be that he loves destruction and chaos (indeed it is indisputable that he sometimes loves them very much) because he is instinctively afraid of achieving his goal and completing the structure he is constructing? How do you know? Maybe he just loves the structure from a distance, and not at all from close up; maybe he only loves to build it, and not to live in it, leaving it afterwards *aux animaux domestiques*,[13] to ants, sheep and the rest of them. Now, ants have different taste entirely. They

have one amazing structure of that kind, which lasts forever
– the anthill.

The respectable species of ants began with the anthill
and they will likely end with the anthill too, which brings
great honour to their constancy and positive nature. But man
is a frivolous and improper being, and perhaps, like a chess
player, he loves only the process of achieving his ends and
not the ends themselves. And who knows (one cannot guar-
antee it) perhaps the sole aim of mankind on earth, for which
he strives, is the perpetual process of achieving, in other words,
in living and not in attainment itself – which can be nothing
other than two-times-two-is-four, a formula that is. However,
two-times-two-is-four, gentlemen, is not living anymore but the
beginning of death. At least, man has always feared this two-
times-two-is-four, and I fear it myself now. Let's say a man has
to do nothing but seek such an equation, crossing the oceans
and giving his life to this quest – but to find it, to really locate
it, oh, Lord, he would be afraid. Indeed, he feels that when
he locates it, there will be nothing left to seek. Workers having
finished their work receive their money at least, and head
to the tavern, then get put in the lock-up for the night – and
that keeps them busy for the week. But where is the rest of
mankind to go? You'll notice, at least, that every time he
achieves an end, there's something awkward about him.
He loves the process of achieving, but does not really like to
have achieved, and that is, of course, terribly funny. In a word,
mankind is a comical construction; there's a big joke in all of
this, obviously. But two-times-two-is-four is nonetheless an insuf-
ferable thing. Two-times-two-is-four, indeed, is simply effrontery,
in my opinion. Two-times-two-is-four looks upon you smugly
as it stands right in your path with arms stretched to either side,
spitting at you. I will agree that two-times-two-is-four is an

excellent thing – but if we're going to go and praise everything then two-times-two-is-five is also sometimes a very lovely little thing.

And why are you so firmly and solemnly convinced that only the normal and the positive – in a word, prosperity alone – is to man's advantage? Is reason perhaps mistaken about man's advantage? Could it be that man doesn't love only prosperity? Maybe he loves suffering just as much. Maybe suffering is equally as advantageous to him as prosperity. Man sometimes fiercely loves suffering, with a passion, and that is a fact. No need to consult world history to confirm that; you can ask yourself, that is if you are a person who has at least lived a little. As far as my personal opinion goes, to love only prosperity is even somehow unseemly. Whether it's good, whether it's bad, it's sometimes very pleasant to smash things apart. Now, I'm not taking a stand here for suffering, nor indeed for prosperity. I am taking a stand . . . for my whims, and that they may be guaranteed to me, when I have need of them. Suffering, for example, is inadmissible in vaudeville, I know that. In a crystal palace, it is even unthinkable: suffering is doubt, negation, and what sort of crystal palace would it be if it contained doubt? All the same, I am convinced that when it comes to real suffering, that is, destruction and chaos, man will never renounce it. Suffering – well, it is the sole determinant of consciousness. I did, though, set out at the beginning that consciousness, in my opinion, is man's greatest misfortune, but I know that man loves it and wouldn't trade it for any gratification. Consciousness, for example, is infinitely greater than two-times-two-is-four. After two-times-two-is-four, it stands to reason that there is nothing left – not only to do, but to know, even. All that you could then do would be to plug up your five senses and plunge into contemplation.

And you will have the same result as you do with conscious-ness, that is you may also have nothing to do, but then at least you can flog yourself occasionally, and that would be stimulating after all. It may be retrograde, but it's still better than nothing.

X

You believe in a crystal palace, eternally indestructible; a palace, that is, at which you could never stick out your tongue furtively, or gesture rudely from inside your pocket. Well, maybe I am afraid of this building exactly because it is crystal and eternally indestructible and that it will be impossible to stick out my tongue at it, even furtively.

Don't you see: if instead of a palace it was a henhouse, and it started to rain, I would perhaps crawl into the henhouse to avoid getting wet, but all the same, I wouldn't take the henhouse for a palace just out of gratitude that it protected me from the rain. You laugh, you are saying that in this case it doesn't matter if it's a henhouse or a mansion. Yes, I answer you, if one is living only in order not to get wet.

But what is to be done if I have taken it into my head that one might live not just for this reason, and that if one must live, one is better off living in a mansion? That is what I want, that is my desire. You will only rake it out of me at the point when you have changed my desires. Well, change them then, attract me with something else, give me another ideal. But meanwhile, I still won't take a henhouse for a palace. Let it be so, that the crystal palace is a pouffe,[14] that it is not viable according to the laws of nature, and that I have invented it only as a result of my own silliness, as a result of certain old non-rational habits of our generation. But what is it to me that it isn't viable? What difference is it to me if it exists in my desires, or, better put, if it exists while my desires exist? Maybe you laugh again? Laugh as you will. I can take any amount of mockery but still I won't say that I am satiated when I am hungry; still I know that I won't settle for a compromise, for a persistent, recurring zero, just because it exists according to the laws of nature and exists *in reality*. I will not accept as the crown of my desires, an apartment building of quarters for poor residents on contracts of a thousand years with 'Wagenheim the Dentist' on a sign by the entrance. Destroy my desires, blot out my ideals, show me something better and I will follow you. You, perhaps, will say that it's not worth getting involved; but in that case then I can answer you with the same again. We are discussing this seriously and if you don't want to favour me with your attention then I won't bow to you. I have the underground.

But while I am still living and desiring, let my hand wither if I bring even one brick to such an apartment building! Disregard the fact that I just rejected the crystal palace for the sole reason that you can't stick your tongue out at it. I didn't say that because I am so given to sticking out my tongue. Perhaps I was angry because to this moment, there isn't one building to be found at which one cannot stick out one's tongue. On the contrary, I would let my tongue be cut off from gratitude alone, if only things could be arranged so that I myself would no longer want to stick it out. What matter is it to me that such a thing can't be arranged and that one must feel satisfied with apartments? Why am I predisposed to such desires? Am I predisposed to them only so I can then come to the conclusion that my whole disposition is nothing but a dupe? Can this be the whole point? I don't believe it.

But you know what, I'm convinced that my brothers of the underground should be kept on a short leash. We may only be able to sit for forty years in the underground, but when we do come out into the light and burst forth, we talk and talk and talk.

XI

The final word, gentlemen: it is better to do nothing! Conscious inertia is better! And so, long live the underground! Even though I said that I envy the normal man with my every last drop of bile, I wouldn't want to be him under the circumstances in which I see him (though I won't stop envying him all the same. No, no, the underground is more advantageous anyway!). There, at least you can . . . Eh! There I go, I'm lying. I'm lying because I know myself, just as two-times-two-is-four, that the underground is not better at all but something different, quite different, for which I thirst but which I am never able to find! Damn the underground!

Now, here's the thing that would be better, that is, if I could believe in at least something of what I've just written. I swear to you, gentlemen, that I don't believe in one, not even one little word of what I have just scribbled! That is, I might believe, but at the same time, who knows why, I feel and I suspect that I am lying like a cobbler.

'Why then have you written all this?' you say to me.

Well, what if I put you away for forty-odd years without

anything to do, and then came back to you forty years later, to the underground, to see where you'd got yourself? Can you really leave a man without anything to do for forty years?

'Isn't it shameful, isn't it humiliating!' you will perhaps say to me, derisively shaking your head. 'You thirst for life and you try to resolve life's questions with a logical mess. And how troublesome, how insolent your escapades, and how scared you are at the same time! You speak nonsense and are satisfied with it; you speak with insolence and are ceaselessly afraid, begging for forgiveness for it. You assert that you are afraid of nothing and at the same time you seek our opinion. You assert that you are gnashing your teeth and at the same time you say witty things to make us laugh. You know that your witticisms are not witty, but you, obviously, are very satisfied with their literary value. You may, perhaps, have happened to actually suffer, but you don't respect your suffering in the slightest. You may have truth in you, too, but you have no virtue; for the pettiest vanity you put your truth on show, to shame, to market. You really want to say something, but out of fear you hide your last word because you lack the resolve to utter it, and have only cowardly impertinence. You boast of consciousness but you only vacillate, because, though your mind works, your heart is murky with depravity, and without a clean heart there will be no full and correct consciousness. And how troublesome you are, how you impose yourself, how you grimace! Lies, lies and lies!'

It goes without saying that I made up all your words myself just now. This, too, is from the underground. I have been listening to you for forty years in a row through a crack in the floor. I thought them up myself, that's all there was to think up. It's no wonder then that I have learned them by heart and that they have taken a literary form.

But can you actually be so gullible as to imagine that I will publish all this and then go on to give it you to read? And another riddle for me: why, actually, do I call you 'gentlemen' why do I even address myself to you as if you were really my readers? Such confessions as I am intending to begin setting forth do not get published and are not being given for others to read. At least, I don't have as much resolution as that to me and I don't see a need for it, either. Do you see: a fantasy has arrived in my head, and I want to realise it at any cost. This is the thing.

There are such things in the reminiscences of every man that he would reveal not to everyone but only to friends. There are also some that he wouldn't reveal to friends, but only to himself, and only in secret. But there are also, finally, things that a man is even afraid to reveal to himself, and these things accrue in sufficient amounts for any decent man. That is to say, the more decent he is, the more of these he has. At least, I myself recently decided to recall some of my past adventures, but until now I have always sought to evade them, with a certain uneasiness even. But now, as I have not only decided to recall them but also even decided to record them, now I specifically want to test something: can one be completely open with oneself and not fear the whole truth? I will note, by the way, that Heine affirms that true autobiography is almost impossible and a man will likely lie about himself. In his opinion, Rousseau, for example, certainly lied about himself in his confessions, and even lied deliberately, out of vanity. I am convinced that Heine is right; I understand very well how sometimes vanity alone can make one slap whole crimes upon oneself, and I can quite easily grasp which kind of vanity it could be. But Heine was judging those who confessed before the public. Whereas I am writing only for myself and will declare once and for all that if I write as though I am addressing a reader it is only just for show, because it is easier for me to write that way. It is a form, just an empty form – I will never have readers. I have already made that clear.

I do not want to feel shy about anything in the compilation of my notes. I will not establish any order or systems. What I recall is what I will write.

Well, for example, someone might seize on a word and ask me, 'if you are really not counting on having readers then why do you make such agreements with yourself, and on paper too, that you won't establish any order or systems, that you'll write what you recall and so on and so on? Why are you explaining yourself? Why are you excusing yourself?'

Now, hold on, I'll give you an answer.

But there is a whole psychology to this. Maybe it is that I am just a coward. But maybe it is that I have intentionally imagined an audience before me so that I may behave more properly, when the time comes to write. There may be a thousand reasons.

And here is another thing: exactly for what and to what end do I want to write? If it isn't for the public then I might as well just recall it all mentally, not translating it to paper.

Yes, sir. But it comes out more augustly on paper. There's something more awesome to it, my judgment upon myself is greater, my style is enhanced. Besides that, I will perhaps actually receive some relief from the writing of it. Just now, for example, I am especially burdened with one ancient memory. I was reminded of it clearly a few days ago and ever since it has remained with me, like an annoying musical motif that just won't let go. And yet I must get it to let go. I have hundreds of memories like it; but now and then one of these hundreds will emerge and weigh upon me. I believe for some reason that if I write it down then it will let go of me. And why not try?

In the end, I'm bored, and I'm constantly doing nothing. Writing will be just like doing work. They say that man becomes good and honest through work. So, here's my chance at least.

Now snow is falling, it's almost wet, yellow, turbid. Yesterday it also snowed and so it did a few days ago, too. It seems to me that the wet snow has reminded me of the anecdote that won't let me go. And so, let this be a story about wet snow.

PART TWO

A STORY ABOUT
WET SNOW

When from the dark of deviation
with burning words of affirmation
I plucked your fallen soul,
And overcome with deep torment,
You cursed the vice, denied consent,
Your hands could not console;
Your principles errant, astray,
Were punished with the memory
Your story as you now relayed
of all that went before me,
And suddenly, with hands on face,
Your tears allowed to fall,
Full of horror and disgrace,
Indignant and appalled . . .
etc. etc. etc.

From a poem by N.A. Nekrasov

I

At the time, I was all of twenty-four years old. My life was gloomy, untidy and solitary to a savage extent. I didn't associate with anyone and even avoided talking, and took more and more frequent refuge in my corner. At my post, in the office, I tried not to glance at anyone, and I was perfectly aware that my colleagues not only considered me an odd fellow but – so it always seemed to me – it was as if they were looking at me with a certain loathing. It occurred to me: why does it not seem to any other man that he is looked upon with loathing? One of our clerks had a repulsive and very pockmarked face, almost criminal even. If I had a face as indecent as his, I don't think I would have dared to look at anyone. Another had such an over-worn uniform that there was a bad smell about him. And yet not one of these gentlemen was embarrassed – not by his clothes, nor by his face, nor in any way morally. Not one nor the other even imagined that they were looked upon with loathing; and if they had imagined it, then it wouldn't have mattered to them, as long as their superiors didn't deign to direct their gaze at them. Now, it is completely clear to me that as a consequence of my boundless vanity, and therefore the standards I ask of myself, I very often looked upon myself with frenzied displeasure, which carried me to loathing, and so I mentally ascribed my own gaze to everyone else. For instance, I hated my face, I found it vile and even suspected that there was some abject expression to it, so that

53

every time I appeared at my post, I desperately tried to carry myself as independently as possible in order not to be suspected of abjection, and I expressed with my face as much nobility as possible. 'My face may be unattractive,' I thought, 'but may it be noble, expressive and, most importantly, *extraordinarily* intelligent.' But, agonisingly, I knew for certain that all these perfections would never be expressed in my face. And most awful of all, I found my face to be positively stupid. I would have absolutely settled for intelligence. I would even have agreed to a face with an abject expression, as long as it was found to be fiercely intelligent at the same time.

It goes without saying that I hated our clerks from the first to the last of them, and I despised them all, as well as being somewhat afraid of them. On occasion I would even suddenly place them above myself. It would happen all of a sudden, somehow: I was either despising them or placing them above me. A cultivated and decent man could not be vain without boundlessly high standards for himself and without despising himself to an extreme of hatred at times. But, whether despising them or placing them above myself, I lowered my eyes at almost every encounter. I even made experiments: would I be able to bear someone's gaze? I was always first to look down. This tormented me into a frenzy. I was also sick with the fear that I was ridiculous and so I slav-ishly observed routine in everything exterior to me. I fell into the common rut with loving affection, and I was scared with all my soul of any eccentricity in myself. But how was I to keep it up? I was morbidly cultivated, as cultivated as is expected of a man of our time. They are all stupid – one and all look the same, like sheep in a herd. Perhaps, I was the only one in the whole office to whom it forever seemed that I was a coward and a slave; and that was precisely because it seemed to me that I was a cultivated man. And it didn't just seem so, but it was in fact so, in reality: I was a coward and a slave. I say this without any embarrassment. Every decent man of our time is and should be a coward and a slave. This is his normal condition. I am deeply convinced of this. He is made thus, and attuned for it. And it isn't just at the present time, due to some happenstance or another, but in general – at all times, a decent man should be a coward and a slave. This is the law of nature for all decent people on the earth. If any one of them happens to pluck up a bit of courage over something, he need not take comfort nor pleasure in it: he will still always take fright at something else. Such is the only perennial outcome. Only donkeys and mules make shows of courage, and only up to a certain wall. It isn't worth paying attention to them because they are of exactly no significance.

There was one other circumstance that tormented me: specifically, that no one was like me and I was like no one else. I am one, and they are *all*, I'd think, and then sink into thought.

It is evident from this that I was still very much a boy then.

There were contradictions, too. Indeed, some of the time it was dreadful to go to the office; it got to the point that many times I went home sick from work. But suddenly, not for any particular reason, a streak of scepticism and indifference set in (I always get streaks like this) and then I would laugh at my own impatience and squeamishness, reproaching myself for my *romanticism*. Either I don't want to talk to anyone, or I go so far not only as to converse but even to consider treating them as friends. All my squeamishness suddenly in one moment, not for any particular reason, would disappear. Who knows, maybe I was never really squeamish and it was only an affectation, something I learnt from books? To this day, I still haven't resolved this question. Once I'd actually made friends with them, started to visit them at home, to play *preference*, drink vodka with them, chat about promotions . . . But allow me here to make a digression.

We, the Russians, generally speaking, have never had such stupid, star-gazing romantics as the Germans and especially the French, who are unmoved by anything – the earth can even shake beneath them, the whole of France can perish at the barricades but they remain the same, and won't change even for decency's sake but carry on with their star-gazing songs to their graves, so to speak, because they are fools. We, on Russian soil, have no fools; that is well known; that is what differentiates us from the other Germanic territories. Consequently, such star-gazing natures cannot be found here in pure form. It was all those 'positive' publicists and critics of ours who went hunting for Konstanzhoglos and Uncle Pyotr Ivanoviches,[15] and who foolishly took them for our ideal, who superimposed it all onto our romantics, conflating them with the kind of star-gazers you find in Germany or France. On the contrary, the characteristics of our romantic are completely and directly the opposite to the star-gazing European type, and not one little European proportion will fit. (Allow me to use this word 'romantic' – it's an ancient little word, a respectable one, which has served well and is well known.) The characteristics of our romantic are to understand everything, *to see everything and to see it often incomparably more clearly than the very most positive of our minds*; our romantic is reconciled with nothing and to no one, but at the same time nothing repels him; he gets around everything; he yields to everything, he is politic towards everyone; never losing sight of his useful, practical goal (such as a little government apartment, a good little pension, a little medal or two), he keeps an eye on this goal through all his enthusiasms and his little tomes of lyrical verses, and at the same time he preserves 'the elevated and the beautiful' inviolately, to his grave, and he preserves himself quite well, too, incidentally, like some precious jewel in cotton wool, if only for the sake of the very same 'elevated and beautiful'. Our romantic is a broad man and the foremost rogue of all our rogues, I can assure you of that . . . from experience, even. Of course, all this is so if the romantic is intelligent. But what am I saying! The romantic is always intelligent, I wanted only to note that though there have been romantic fools among us, they don't count and they were uniquely so because in the prime of their lives they reincarnated as Germans, and in order to preserve more easily their little jewel, they settled somewhere over there, likely in Weimar or in the Schwartzwald. For instance, I sincerely despised my service but I didn't spit upon it, out of necessity, because I was sitting there and receiving money for it. As a result – take note – I didn't spit upon it. Our romantic would sooner go out of his mind (which, however, very rarely happens) than start spitting unless some other career was in view, and he would never be chased away with a shove but might be taken off to the mad house in the form of the 'King of Spain'[16] and that is only if he were to go very mad. But here in Russia it is only the thin ones and the pale ones that go out of their minds. A countless number of romantics subsequently attain considerable rank. What remarkable versatility! And what a capacity for the most contradictory of sensations! I was comforted by this back then, and have those same thoughts today. Why do we have such a lot of 'broad natures' who never lose their ideals, even before their very final fall; and though they won't stir a finger for their ideals, and though they are inveterate villains and thieves, they are tearfully devoted to their first ideal and extraordinarily honest in their souls. Yes, sirs, it is only here that the most inveterate scoundrel can be completely and even exaltedly honest in his soul and at the same time never cease to be a scoundrel. I will repeat, time and again our romantics turn out to be such accomplished rogues (I use the word 'rogue' lovingly), displaying such a quick grasp of reality and positive knowledge that their amazed superiors and the public can only click their tongues at them in stupefaction. Their versatility is truly amazing, and God knows what it will turn into, and how it will develop in subsequent circumstances, and what it promises us in times to come. It isn't bad material, sirs! And I'm not speaking out of any patriotism, funny or fermented! But I am sure that again you're thinking that I am jesting. Who knows, maybe it's the opposite, which is that you're sure that I really do think all this. In any case, gentlemen, I will consider either of your opinions as an honour and with especial pleasure. And forgive me for my digression.

It goes without saying that I didn't maintain friendships with my colleagues and was very soon spitting in their direction and due to my erstwhile youthful inexperience I even stopped greeting them, I just cut them off. This, however, only happened to me once. In general, I was always alone.

First of all, at home, I read more than anything. I wanted to deaden all that was constantly boiling inside me with external sensations. And of all available external sensations, the only one for me was reading. Reading, of course, helped a lot – it excited, pleasured and tormented. But at times it bored me terribly. After all, I still wanted to do something. I suddenly plunged into dark, subterranean, nasty – not vice but mini-vice. The little passions in me were sharp and burning from my perpetual, sickly irritability. There were outbursts, hysterical, convulsive, with tears. Apart from reading, there was nowhere to go – that is, there was nothing that I could at the time respect in my surroundings and to which I was attracted. In addition to that, sorrow was starting to boil within me; an hysterical thirst for contradiction and contrast arrived, and so I succumbed to debauchery. Indeed, I haven't said all this now merely in order to justify myself . . . But no! I lie! I did do it to justify myself. I am making this little observation for myself, gentlemen. I don't want to lie. I gave my word.

I engaged in debauchery in solitude, at night, secretly, fearfully, dirtily, with a shame that didn't leave me at the most appalling moments – moments when it even reached a point of damnation. I was already carrying the underground in my soul. I was terribly afraid that somehow I would be seen, be met, be recognised. I went between a variety of very dark places.

Once, passing at night by a certain tavern, through a lighted window I saw a group of gentlemen fighting with billiard cues, and then one of them was thrown through the window. At another time this would have been abominable to me but then, suddenly, the moment arrived when I rather envied the thrown man, and envied him so much that I even went into the tavern to the billiards room. Perhaps, I said to myself, I'll get into a fight and they'll throw me through a window, too.

I wasn't drunk, but what would you have me do – this is the degree of hysteria to which sorrow might consume you! But nothing came of it. It seemed that I wasn't even able to jump through a window and I left, not having fought.

I had been put in my place by an officer from the first moment. I was standing at the billiards table and without realising it I was blocking the way, and he needed to get past; he took me by the shoulders and silently – without warning me, without explaining himself – moved me from the place where I stood to another place, and then walked on as though he had noticed nothing. I would have forgiven a punch, but I couldn't at all forgive him for transplanting and so definitively failing to notice me.

The devil knows what I would have then given for a real, a more correct argument – a more proper, more *literary* one, so to speak! I had been treated like a fly. This officer was some ten *vershok*[17] in height. And I am short and skinny. The argument, however, was in my hands: was it worth protesting, and of course then being thrown through the window? I thought about it again and preferred . . . to retire into the background, embittered.

I left the tavern confused and agitated, went straight home, and the next day I continued my debauchery, more timidly, more cowed, more miserably than before, with tears in my eyes as it were, but continued just the same. Don't think, however, that I was cowardly before the officer out of cowardice: I have never been a coward in my soul, even though I have constantly behaved like a coward in real life but – wait, don't laugh, there's an explanation for this; I have an explanation for everything, rest assured.

Oh, if only this officer had been the type to agree to a duel! But no, he was one of those gentlemen (alas! a long disappeared sort), who prefer to act with billiard cues or, like Gogol's Lieutenant Pirogov, by calling upon the authorities. They didn't fight duels anyway, and in any case they would have considered a duel with the likes of me, a lowly staffer, inappropriate. In general they considered a duel to be something inconceivable, freethinking and French – but they caused enough offence themselves, especially those who were about ten *vershok* in height.

I didn't cow out of cowardice but out of utter unbounded vanity. I wasn't frightened of his six-foot self, nor of the painful beating I would get, nor of being thrown through the window. My physical bravery really would have sufficed. But my moral bravery was lacking. I was frightened that everyone present – from the impudent *marker* to the last, rotten, pimply little clerk with his greasy collar – would fail to understand and would ridicule me when I started protesting and speaking with them in literary language. Since, to this day, when it comes to a point of honour – that is to say, not honour but a point of honour (*point d'honneur*) – one cannot possibly speak in anything other than literary language. Ordinary language never refers to a 'point of honour'. I was completely sure (a sense of reality, never mind all that romanticism!) that they would all simply burst from laughing, and that the officer wouldn't just beat me up, that is inoffensively, but would definitely start shoving me around with his knee, leading me in this manner around the billiards table, and only after that would he have mercy and throw me through the window. Of course, I wouldn't let this meagre story end there for me. Afterwards, I often encountered this officer on the street and took particular note of him. Only I don't know if he recognised me. Probably not. I conclude this from certain signals. But I . . . I watched him with spite and hatred, and so it continued . . . for several years! My spite even strengthened and grew with the years. At first, I started quietly to learn about this officer. It was hard for me, because I wasn't acquainted with anyone. But one day someone cried out his surname on the street when I was walking behind him at a distance as though fastened to him, and that's how I learned his surname. Another time I followed him right up to his apartments and in exchange for a *grivennik*[18] I found out from the porter where he lived, on which floor, alone or with someone and so on. In a word, all that you might learn from a porter. Once, in the morning, though I have never litera-turised, I suddenly had the thought to describe him in a satirical fashion, in a caricature, in the form of a short story. I wrote this story with pleasure. I satirised and even slandered him a little; at first I slightly changed his surname, so you could recognise it straight away, but then, after ripe consid-eration, I changed it and sent it to *Notes of the Fatherland*. But they didn't publish satires at the time and my story wasn't printed. This was very vexing to me. Sometimes spite just choked me. In the end, I decided to challenge my opponent to a duel. I composed a beautiful and enticing letter to him, begging him to apologise to me; in the case of refusal, I rather solidly hinted at a duel. The letter was composed such that if the officer had a slight understanding of the 'elevated and the beautiful', then he would have certainly run to me in order to throw his arms around me and proffer friendship. And how good that would have been! Together we would have really lived! Really lived! He would have protected me with my high ranking; I would have ennobled him with my developed mind, and well . . . ideas, and there's a lot else that might have been!

Imagine, by then two years had gone by since he had offended me, and my challenge was a most outrageous anach-ronism, despite the dexterity of my letter, which explained and obscured the anachronism. But, thank God (I've been thanking the Almighty with tears in my eyes ever since) I never sent my letter. A frost comes over my skin when I think about how it might have turned out if I'd sent it.

But suddenly, suddenly I got my revenge in the most simple, the most genius of ways! The brightest thought struck me. Sometimes, on a holiday, I would stroll along Nevsky at about four o'clock, walking on the sunny side of the street. That is, I wasn't walking at all, I was experiencing innumerable torments, humiliations and outpourings of bile; but that was probably just what I needed. I darted around like a carp, in the most unattractive way, in between the passers by, repeatedly giving way, sometimes to generals, other times to cavalier guards and hussars, and to ladies, too. I felt convulsive pains in my heart at these moments and a heat in my spine at the singular idea of the *misère* of my attire, the *misère* and vulgarity of my darting little figure. This was a torturous torture, a ceaseless unbearable humiliation born of the thought, which became a continuous and spontaneous thought, that I was a fly before this whole world, a nasty, obscene fly – more clever, more cultured, more noble than everyone, that is a given – but a fly who endlessly steps aside for others, is humiliated by all and is insulted by everyone. Why did I inflict this torture upon myself, why did I walk along Nevsky? I don't know. But I was simply *drawn* there at every opportunity.

Even then I had started to experience the surges of pleasure about which I spoke in the first chapter. After the story with the officer I was even more powerfully drawn to that place: on Nevsky I encountered him more than anywhere, and it was there that I admired him. He also went there, mostly on holidays. He too, even, gave way to generals and to the especially high-ranked, and he also wound his way around them like a carp; but people of my sort, or even those a bit more polished than my sort – he just trampled them. He went straight at them as though there was an empty space before him, and he wouldn't give way under any circumstances.

I became intoxicated with spite, looking upon him, and bitterly stepped aside for him every time. It tormented me that I couldn't even be on an equal footing with him on the street. 'Why must you invariably be the one to step aside?' I insisted on asking myself, in wild hysterics, waking sometimes at three o'clock in the morning to ask this. 'Why is it always you and not him? Indeed there's no rule about it, and is it written anywhere that this should be so? So let it be fair, as usually happens when refined people meet each other: he will step aside partly and you will do so partly also, and you will pass each other, mutually respecting each other.' But it wasn't so, and nonetheless, it was I who stepped aside, and he didn't even notice that I stepped aside for him. And here is the most surprising thought that suddenly dawned on me. And what, I wondered, if when I encounter him . . . I don't move to one side? Not moving to one side on purpose, even if it means that I bump into him. Well, how would that be? This bold idea slowly took hold of me such that it would give me no peace. I dreamed about it continuously, and I walked along Nevsky with terror and purpose in order to imagine even more clearly how I would accomplish this, when I would do it. I was in ecstasy. This plan seemed to me more and more likely and possible. Of course, I won't push him, really, I thought, softened by the pleasure of it in advance, but I just won't stand aside, I'll collide with him, not so that it's very painful but just like that, shoulder to shoulder, just exactly enough as is deemed proper; so that I shall bump into him as much as he bumps into me. I was finally, totally decided on it. But preparations took a very long time. First of all, for the moment of this performance I should appear in more respectable form and should pay attention to my attire. In any case, if, for example, a public incident was incited (and the public here

is *superflu*:[20] there goes the countess, there goes Prince D. and
there goes the whole of literature), I must be well dressed.
This is suggestive and immediately gives us equal footing in
some way in the eyes of high society. With this in mind, I
drew my salary in advance and bought black gloves and a
proper hat from Churkin's. Black gloves seemed to me more
respectable, more *bon ton*[21] than the lemon-coloured ones that
I had fallen upon initially. The colour is too sharp, too much
as though one hopes to stand out, I decided, and so I didn't
take the lemon-coloured ones. I had already long ago prepared
a good shirt with white bone studs; but my overcoat detained
me for some time. In and of itself, my overcoat wasn't bad at
all, it kept me warm; but it was cotton and the collar was
raccoon, which constituted the height of servility. I had to
change the collar no matter what and replace it with beaver
as the officers had it. For this I began going to Gostiny Dvor[22]
and after several attempts I homed in on one, a cheap German
beaver. These German beavers, they wear out and take on a
paltry look very quickly, but to start off with, when they are
newly bought, they look very acceptable indeed, and at this
point I only needed it for one particular occasion. I asked the
price: it was expensive nonetheless. After some fundamental
reasoning, I decided to sell my raccoon collar.

I still required a sum of money, which was significant for
me, and I decided to take it on loan from Anton Antonich
Setochkin, my superior, a meek person, though serious and
positive, who hasn't given money on loan to anyone, but to
whom I was once, when stepping up to my post, especially
recommended by an important person who had appointed me
for service. I tormented myself terribly. Asking Anton Antonich
for money seemed monstrous and shameful to me. I didn't sleep
for two or three nights, and barely slept at all back then – I

was in a fever. My heart seemed to wane and then suddenly
started to jump, jump, jump! Anton Antonich was at first
surprised and then he frowned, then reflected on it, and gave
me the loan anyway, taking from me a receipt giving him the
right to receive the sum he had paid me in two weeks' time,
from my salary. With this, everything was finally ready. My
handsome beaver usurped the filthy raccoon and I started
to set to my task little by little. It wouldn't have been right to
resolve this on impulse, that would have been in vain. This
matter needed to be handled skilfully, and indeed little by
little. But I'll confess that after many attempts, even I started
to despair: how were we to bump into each other? We couldn't
just bump into each other – if only! Whether I was making
preparations or setting intentions, it seemed that we would
bump into each other at any moment, but again, I would step
aside and he would walk past without noticing me. I even said
prayers as I walked up to him, so that God would instill me
with resolve. One time I had really resolved myself but it ended
with me falling at his feet because at the very last moment, at
about two *vershok* distance from him, my courage suddenly
lacked. He very calmly advanced at me, and I, like a ball, flew
off to the side. That night I was ill again with fever and
delirium. But then, suddenly, everything was concluded as well
as it could have been. The night before, I finally settled on
the idea that I would not go through with my pernicious intentions and decided it was all to no avail, and with that end in
mind I went out for the last time onto Nevsky only in order
to have a look for myself – how would it be to no avail?
Suddenly, at three paces from my enemy, I unexpectedly
committed myself, squeezed my eyes shut and – we solidly
bumped into each other, shoulder to shoulder! I didn't step
aside even one *vershok* and walked past him on an even

footing! He didn't look around and made as if he hadn't noticed; but he was only pretending, I am sure of this. To this day I am sure of this! It stands to reason that I caught the worst of it – he was stronger – but that was beside the point. The point was that I attained my goal, I had maintained my dignity, not stepping even a pace aside, and I had publicly set myself on an equal social footing with him. I turned around to go home having avenged myself for everything completely. I was in ecstasy. I celebrated and sang Italian arias. I won't describe for you what happened to me three days later – it stands to reason – but if you have read my first chapter 'The Underground' then you can guess it for yourself. The officer was then transferred somewhere; I haven't seen him for about fourteen years at this point. What's my good fellow doing now? Whom is he now trampling?

II

And so my depraved streak ended and I became terribly nauseous. Remorse would set in and I would chase it away: I was too nauseous. Little by little, however, I grew used to it. I grew used to everything, that is, I didn't just grow used to it, but somehow I voluntarily agreed to endure it. But I had a way out, it reconciled everything, it was to escape into 'all that is elevated and beautiful' – in my dreams, of course. I dreamed terribly, I dreamed for three months in a row, taking refuge in my corner, and I can assure you that at these moments I didn't resemble that gentleman who, in the confusion of his chicken heart, had sewn a German beaver to the collar of his coat. I suddenly turned into a hero. I wouldn't even have admitted my ten-*vershok*-tall lieutenant, had he called on me. I couldn't even picture him in my mind. What dreams they were and how I could be satisfied by them – it's hard for me to say now, but at the time I was satisfied by them. Even now, though, I am satisfied by them to some extent. My dreams were especially sweet and they came stronger to me after all that depravity, they came to me with remorse and tears, with curses and ecstasies. There were moments of such positive rapture, such happiness, that I swear I could not sense even the tiniest bit of contempt within me, really and truly. There was faith, hope, love. And that is the point – I blindly believed then that by some sort of miracle, some sort of external circumstance would suddenly push everything aside, open everything wide; suddenly a horizon of appropriate behaviours would appear, benevolent, beautiful and most importantly, poised for action (what kind of behaviour, exactly, I never knew but most importantly they were poised for action) and then I would suddenly step out into the divine light of day, practically riding a white steed and wearing a laurel crown. I couldn't conceive of taking second place and that was exactly why I was peaceful with occupying last place. Either hero or filth, there was no middle ground. This was my undoing, because in my filth I comforted myself with the fact that I was a hero at the same time, and that the hero in me was hidden under the filth: for the ordinary man, say, it is shameful to get filthy but the hero is too sublime to become completely filthy, therefore he is allowed some filth. It's remarkable that these surges of the 'elevated and the beautiful' came to me even during times of depravity – it was exactly at moments when I would reach rock bottom that I felt it, in distinct spurts, as though it was reminding me of itself. It did not, however, eliminate the debauchery with its appearance. On the contrary, it was as though it enlivened the depravity with contrast and came in exactly the amount that was needed to make a good sauce. This sauce consisted of contradictions and sufferings, of torturous inner analysis, and all these torments and bedevilments added a certain spice, so that even the thought of my depravity, in a word, fulfilled the requirements of a good sauce. All this was not without a certain profundity. Could I really have agreed to a simple, vulgar, spontaneous, pen-pushing, little bit of depravity and borne all this filth upon myself? What about it could have charmed me and lured me out onto the streets at night? No, I had a dignified escape clause for everything.

But how much love, oh Lord, how much love I experienced in those dreams of mine, in those 'flights into all that is beautiful and elevated': and though it may have been fantastical love, and never assigned to any human reality, there was so much of it, this love, that afterwards, in reality, I felt there was no need even to have it assigned – that would have been an excessive luxury. Everything, though, always ended happily with a lazy and intoxicating transition to the arts, that is, to beautiful forms of being, perfectly prepared, vigorously stolen from poets and novelists and adapted for all manner of service and bidding. For example, I am triumphant over everyone; everyone else, of course, is covered in dust and they are obliged to voluntarily recognise all of my perfections, and I forgive them all. I fall in love, poet and courtier that I am. I receive incalculable millions and immediately sacrifice them to humankind while I confess my disgraces before all people, which of course aren't just disgraces but include a great deal of that which is 'beautiful and elevated,' something of the Manfredian.[23] Everyone weeps and kisses me (otherwise, they would be taken for idiots), and I walk, barefoot and hungry, to preach new ideas and to break up the reactionaries at Austerlitz. Then a march would be played, an amnesty would be issued, the Pope would agree to exit Rome for Brazil; then there would be a ball for the whole of Italy at the Villa Borghese, which is at the shores of Lake Como, since Lake Como would be transferred to Rome just for this event; then there would be a scene in the bushes, and so on, and so on – as if you didn't know! You will say that it's vulgar and base to put all this on display, after all the raptures and tears to which I confessed. But what makes it base, sirs? You can't really think that I am ashamed of all this and that all this was sillier than anything that may have happened in your lives, gentlemen? And furthermore, believe me that some of it wasn't altogether badly fashioned . . . not everything happened at the shores of Lake Como. But then, you are right; it is actually vulgar and base. And most base of all was that I just now started to justify myself before you. And even more base is that I am now making this remark. Enough already, or this will never end: every thing will be more base than the next.

I didn't have the constitution to dream for more than three months in a row and I started to feel an insurmountable need to dash back into society. For me, dashing into society meant going to visit my superior Anton Antonich Setochkin. He has been the only constant acquaintance of my whole life and even I am surprised by this circumstance. But I only went to him during those times when such a streak set in and my dreams had reached a sufficient state of happiness that it was necessary to quickly embrace people and the whole of human-kind; for this, one needed to have at least one person to hand, someone who actually existed. However, one had to make an appearance at Anton Antonich's on a Tuesday (his day), and therefore one had always to adjust the necessity to embrace the whole of humankind so that it happened on a Tuesday. This Anton Antonich resided at Five Corners, on the fourth floor, in four small rooms, low-ceilinged and each smaller than the next, with an economical and yellowish look to them. He had two daughters, and their aunt poured the tea. The daughters – one was thirteen and the other was fourteen years old – they were both little snub-noses and they embarrassed me terribly because they were always whispering to each other and giggling. Our host usually sat in his study, on a leather sofa in front of a table, together with some grey-haired guest, an official from our department or some other person. I never saw more than two or three guests there, and they were always the same ones. They chatted about excise duty, about an exchange in the Senate, about salaries, about promotions, about His Excellency and how to gain his favour, etc., etc. I had the patience to sit like a fool among these people, listening to them for four hours or so, myself not daring or able to speak up. I turned stupid, several times I took to perspiring, a paralysis descended upon me; but this was good and useful. Upon returning home I was able to set aside my desire to embrace all of humankind for a certain time.

I had, however, another acquaintance, it seemed: Simonov, my old schoolmate. I probably had many schoolmates in Petersburg but I didn't associate with them and had even stopped greeting them in the street. I may have even transferred to another department in order not to be in the same one as them and to sever myself in one blow from my hateful childhood. Curses on that school and all those terrible, punitive years! In a word, I immediately separated myself from those schoolmates as soon as I emerged with my freedom.

There remained two or three people with whom I exchanged greetings upon encountering them. Among them was Simonov, who hadn't differentiated himself in any way at school – he was equable and quiet – but I did determine a certain independence of character, and even honesty in him. I don't think that he was particularly limited, even. At one time we spent some rather bright moments together, but they didn't last long and they were quickly clouded over. He, it seems, felt oppressed by these reminiscences, and it seems, was always afraid that I would slip into that same old tone. I suspected that I was very repulsive to him, but I went and visited him all the same, not knowing this for sure.

Once, on a Thursday, unable to sustain my solitude and knowing that on Thursdays Anton Antonich's door is closed, I was reminded of Simonov. Climbing up to his fourth floor, I particularly thought about the fact that this gentleman found me oppressive and that it was a mistake for me to go there. But since such considerations always, as though deliberately, have the effect of inciting me to clamber further into an ambiguous situation, I went in. It was almost a year since last I had seen Simonov.

III

I found two more of my old schoolmates with him. It looked as if they were discussing a certain important matter. Not one of them paid a shred of attention to my arrival, which was strange because I hadn't seen them for years. It was evident that they considered me to be something akin to a common fly. They hadn't even treated me like that at school, even though everyone there hated me. Of course, I understood that they must be disdainful of me now for the lack of success in my civil service career and for the fact that I had very much let myself go, was badly dressed and so on, and that in their eyes constituted an advertisement of my inaptitude and negligible significance. But I still didn't expect such a degree of contempt. Simonov was surprised at my arrival. In the past, too, he had always seemed surprised at my arrival. All of this perplexed me; I sat down with a certain melancholy and started to listen to what they were discussing.

The conversation was serious, heated even. It was about a farewell dinner, which these gentlemen wanted to set up the following day for their comrade Zverkov, an army officer who was leaving for a distant province. Monsieur Zverkov had been with me at school throughout. I had particularly come to hate him in the latter years. In the earlier years he was just a pretty and frisky boy whom everyone liked. He did consistently badly and the further along we got, the worse he did; but he finished school successfully because he had good connections. In his last year at our school he came into an inheritance, two hundred souls, and since almost everyone there was poor, he made a fanfare of it before of us. He was a vulgarian of a high order, but, however, a good fellow, even when he would do his fanfaring. Despite our superficial, fantastical and bombastic notions of honour and glory, everyone, apart from a small few, fawned over Zverkov the more he bragged. And it wasn't even for their own benefit that they fawned over him, but just because he was a person that was favoured with the gifts of nature. Furthermore, it was somehow accepted that Zverkov was a specialist in the areas of finesse and good manners. This last fact enraged me especially. I hated the frisky, self-assured sound of his voice, how he adored his own witticisms, which came out of him sounding terribly stupid, even though he was bold with language. I hated his handsome but silly face (I would, however, have been inclined to trade my *intelligent* one for it) and his casual manner, in the style of officers of the Forties. I hated the fact that he described his future successes with women (he decided not to start up with women until he had his officer's epaulettes, awaiting them with impatience) and discussed the fact that he would be fighting duels without reprieve. I remember how I, always quiet, suddenly fastened onto Zverkov when he was once talking during a school break with his friends about his future dalliances, and growing as playful as a puppy in the sun, and he suddenly announced that not one of the peasant girls in his village would be spared his attentions, and that this was his *droit de seigneur*,[24] and if the *muzhiks* had the audacity to protest they would all be flogged and all the bearded scoundrels would have their quit-rent doubled. Our louts applauded him but I grappled with him and not out of compassion for the girls and their fathers but simply because such an insect was being applauded. I triumphed on that occasion, but Zverkov, though silly, was also cheerful and impudent, and so he laughed it off, and did so in such a way that I hadn't triumphed after all: the laughter remained on his side. Afterwards, he conquered over me several times, without spite, but easily, jokingly, in passing, laughing. Maliciously and contemptuously, I didn't offer a retort. At graduation, he seemed to make steps towards me; I didn't rebuff him, because it flattered me; but we soon after naturally parted ways. Then I heard about his success as a lieutenant in the barracks, about how he *caroused*. After that, there were other rumours – of his *success* in the service. He didn't greet me in the street, and I suspected that he was afraid of compromising himself, exchanging bows with such an insignificant personage as me. I also saw him once at the theatre, in the third tier, already wearing aiguillettes. He was twisting and bowing before the daughters of an ancient general. In three years he had very much let himself go, even though just as before he was handsome and savvy enough; but he had somehow puffed up and started to become lardy; it was obvious that he would be totally flabby by the age of thirty. And it was for this, Zverkov's final departure, that our comrades wanted to give a dinner. They had gone about with him constantly in the last three years, though even they didn't consider themselves to be on an equal footing to him, I am sure of it.

One of Simonov's two guests was Ferfichkin, a Russified German of short height with the face of a monkey, a mocking fool, my nastiest enemy since early schooldays, a vulgar, impertinent braggart who played at being most delicately conceited but was of course a little coward to his depths. He was among the worshippers of Zverkov, who played up to him with ulterior motives and often borrowed money from him. Simonov's other guest, Trudolyubov, was an unremarkable personage, a military fellow, tall, with a cold physiognomy, rather honest, but one who bowed down before success of all kinds and was only capable of discussing promotions. He was some kind of distant relative of Zverkov's and this, it is silly to say, accorded him a certain significance among us. He always thought little of me; he behaved towards me not exactly politely but tolerably.

'So, now, with seven roubles each,' said Trudolyubov, 'between the three of us that's twenty-one roubles – and for that you can dine well. Zverkov, of course, won't pay.'

'Yes, of course, we'll be inviting him,' Simonov resolved.

'You can't really think,' Ferfichkin meddled haughtily and fervently, just like an obnoxious lackey who boasts about his master the general's medals, 'you don't really think that Zverkov will let us pay for him? He will accept out of delicacy but he'll lay on a half-dozen bottles himself.'

'What will we do with a half-dozen between four?' Trudolyubov remarked, paying attention only to the question of the half-dozen bottles.

'So that's three of us, with Zverkov makes four, twenty-one roubles at the Hôtel de Paris, tomorrow at five o'clock,' Simonov concluded, finally, having been picked as the master of ceremonies.

'How's that twenty-one roubles?' I asked with a certain agitation, acting as though I was offended. 'If you count me too then it wouldn't be twenty-one but twenty-eight roubles.'

It seemed to me that my sudden and unexpected proposal would seem quite gracious and they would all be convinced at once, and would look upon me with respect.

'So you want to join?' Simonov remarked with displeasure, somehow avoiding looking at me. He knew me by heart.

And it drove me wild that he knew me by heart.

'And why not, sir? It seems I'm also a friend, and I confess that I was offended to be excluded,' I said, starting to seethe again.

'And where should we have found you?' Ferfichkin jumped in, rudely.

'You were always at odds with Zverkov,' added Trudolyubov, frowning.

But I had already latched on and wouldn't let it go.

'It seems to me that no one has the right to judge,' I retorted with a tremble in my voice, as though God-knows-what had happened. 'It may be exactly because we used to be at odds that I want to join you now.'

'Well, who can make you out . . . with such lofty ideas.' Trudolyubov smirked.

'We'll add your name,' Simonov decided, addressing me. 'Tomorrow at five o'clock at Hôtel de Paris; don't be mistaken.'

'And the money!' Ferfichkin began in a half-voice, nodding towards me while looking at Simonov, but he stopped short since even Simonov was embarrassed.

'Enough,' said Trudolyubov, standing up. 'If he wants to come that much then let him come.'

'But it's our own little circle of friends,' spat Ferfichkin, also taking up his hat. 'This isn't an official assembly. Maybe we don't want you at all.'

They left. Ferfichkin did not bow to me at all as he left. Trudolyubov barely nodded at me, without glancing. Simonov, with whom I remained face to face, was in some sort of vexed bewilderment and looked at me strangely. He wasn't sitting down and didn't invite me to, either.

'Hm . . . yes . . . so, tomorrow. Will you pay your money now? I, well, so I know for sure,' he muttered, embarrassed.

I blushed, but in blushing I remembered that I had a debt of fifteen roubles to Simonov from time immemorial, which I had never forgotten but had also never paid.

'You will agree yourself, Simonov, that I couldn't have known in coming here . . . and I'm very vexed that I forgot . . .'

'Fine, fine, it doesn't matter. You can pay tomorrow after dinner. I was just, so I knew . . . Please don't . . .'

He stopped short and started to pace the room with even more vexation. In pacing, he started to press on his heels and to stomp harder and harder.

'I'm not keeping you, am I?' I asked after a two-minute silence.

'Oh no!' he suddenly gave a start. 'That is, in truth, yes. You see, I still need to visit someone. It's not far from here,' he added in a kind of apologetic voice and somewhat ashamedly.

'Oh, good God! Why didn't you say something!' I cried, grabbing my cap with a surprised but casual air, which swooped in from God knows where.

'It's not far at all, a couple of steps . . .' Simonov repeated, leading me to the entrance with a bustling air, which didn't suit him at all. 'So, tomorrow at five o'clock sharp!' he yelled after me in the stairway: he was very satisfied that I was leaving. I was in a fury.

What possessed me, what possessed me to launch myself at them? I gnashed my teeth as I walked down the street. And for that scoundrel, that little swine Zverkov! Of course, I shouldn't go; of course, I spit at it: what, am I really bound to go? Tomorrow I will notify Simonov by municipal post.

But that's why I was furious, because I knew for sure that I'd go; and that I would go with purpose; and the more tact-less it was, the more inappropriate it was to go, the sooner I would go.

And there was even a positive obstacle to my going: no money. All in all I had nine roubles. But I needed to give seven of them tomorrow as salary to Apollon, my servant, who lived with me and got seven roubles not including grub.

And it was impossible not to pay him, given Apollon's character. But I will speak later about that *canaille*, about that ulcer of mine.

That said, I knew that I wouldn't pay him, and would go along for certain.

That night I had the ugliest dreams. It's no wonder: the whole evening I had been oppressed by the memories of the punishing years of my school life and I couldn't shake them off. It was my distant relatives on whom I was dependant and about whom I have had no knowledge since, they had sent me to that school. They sent me there, an orphaned, already browbeaten, already pensive, silent boy who looked around wildly at everything. My schoolmates greeted me with spiteful and pitiless mockery for the fact that I wasn't like any of them in the slightest. But I couldn't bear the mockery; I couldn't get on with them as cheaply as they were able to with each other. I hated them straight away and shut myself away from them in fearful, wounded and excessive pride. Their vulgarity outraged me. They laughed cynically to my face, at my awkward figure; meanwhile what stupid faces some of them had! Facial expressions in our school seemed in particular to grow stupider and to degenerate. How many handsome boys went there. After a few years they were disgusting to look at. Even at sixteen years old I morosely marvelled at them; even then, I was astounded at the pettiness of their thinking, the stupidity of their activities, games, conversations. They didn't understand any essential things, weren't interested in any inspiring, striking subjects, so much so that I couldn't help but begin to consider them to be below me. It wasn't insulted vanity that incited me to this, and, for God's sake, don't come out with any nauseating official objections that 'I was only dreaming whereas they understood real life at that time.' They didn't understand a thing, nothing of real life, and I swear this made me even more outraged at them. On the contrary, they perceived the most obvious, blinding reality in a fantastically stupid way and they had already then become used to worshipping success. If something was just but oppressed and downtrodden, they laughed at it cruel-heartedly and igno-miniously. They understood rank for intelligence; at sixteen years of age they were already talking about cosy little jobs. Of course, much of this was due to stupidity, due to bad examples that had surrounded them constantly throughout their childhood and adolescence. They were depraved to a monstrous degree. It goes without saying that this was mostly for appearances, mostly affected cynicism; it goes without saying that youth and a certain freshness twinkled in them, even out of their depravity; but this freshness, even, was not attractive in them and it manifested a sort of profligacy. I hated them terribly, even though, perhaps, I was worse than them. They paid me back in kind and didn't conceal their loathing of me. But I already didn't desire their friendship; on the contrary, I continuously thirsted after their humiliation. In order to rid myself of their mockeries I purposefully started to study as best I could and fought my way through to being among the top pupils. This impressed them. Furthermore, they all started little by little to understand that I had already read such books that they couldn't even begin to read, and to understand such things (that didn't enter into the syllabus of our particular course) about which they hadn't even heard. They looked upon this savagely and mockingly but they were morally in awe, and even the more so since the teachers were paying me atten-tion because of it. The mockeries ceased but the hostility remained and cold, strained relations were established. In the end, I myself couldn't bear it: over the years a need for people, for friends, developed. I tried to start to get closer to others; but always my getting closer turned out to be unnatural and it would come to an end of itself. Once, it seemed, I had a friend. But I was already a despot in my soul; I wanted to govern unbounded over his soul; I wanted to instill in him derision for his surroundings; I demanded from him an arrogant and conclusive severance from our surroundings. I frightened him with the passion of my friendship; I brought him to tears, to convulsions; he was a naive boy and a soul surrenderer. But when he had given himself to me totally, I immediately started to hate him and push him away – as if he was only necessary to me in order to have held a victory over him, only to see him subjugated. But I couldn't conquer everyone; my friend was also unlike any of the others and constituted a most rare exception. The first thing I did when I graduated from school was to abandon the special assignation to which I had been destined, in order to sever all threads, to damn my past and scatter the dust of it. The devil knows why after all that I would drag myself off to Simonov's!

In the morning I snatched myself out of bed early, jumping up with agitation, as if it was all about to start to happen right away. But then, I believed that I was on the verge, on the very verge today of some kind of radical turning point in my life. It was from lack of habit, perhaps, that all my life, in the face of an external event, minute though it may have been, it always seemed that I was right then on the verge of some kind of radical turning point in my life. I went off, however, to work as per usual but then slipped away to go home two hours early in order to get ready. 'The main thing,' I thought, 'is that I should not arrive first, or else they'll think that I am overjoyed to be there.' But there were a thousand of such 'main things', and they all excited me to the point of debility. I polished my boots with my own hands for the second time that day; nothing in the world would impel Apollon to polish them for a second time

in one day – he would find that to be an undue request. I
polished them, having stolen the brushes from the entrance
hall, so that he wouldn't notice and wouldn't then despise
me. Then, I carefully looked over my clothes and found that
everything looked old, shabby and worn-out. I had become
too scruffy. My uniform, maybe, was in good order, but I
couldn't go to dinner in my uniform. And most importantly,
my trousers had a huge yellow stain right on the knee. I
foresaw that this stain alone would subtract nine tenths of
my personal merit. I also knew that it was very base of me
to think like that. But this is no time for thinking; now is
time for reality, I thought, and lost heart. I also knew very
well at that point that I was monstrously exaggerating all
these facts; but what was there to do? I couldn't control
myself any longer and I was trembling with fever. With
despair, I imagined how condescendingly and coldly that
rascal Zverkov would greet me; the dull, ever-irresistible
scorn with which that dullard Trudolyubov would look upon
me; how nastily and impertinently that little insect Ferfichkin
would snigger, at my expense, to worm himself into Zverkov's
favour; how perfectly Simonov would see all this and how
he would despise me for the abjectness of my vanity and my
faint-heartedness, and most importantly, how petty, *unliterary*
and ordinary it would all be. Of course, it would be better
not to go altogether. But this was more impossible than
anything: when I start to be drawn to something I am already
pulled in all the way up to my head. I would have mocked
myself forever after. 'So, you shrunk away, shrunk away from
reality, shrunk away!' On the contrary, I passionately wanted
to prove to all that 'riff-raff' that I wasn't at all the coward
I seemed. And moreover, in the most powerful paroxysms of
my cowardly fever I dreamed of gaining the upper hand,

conquering them, fascinating them, making them love me – if only 'for the sublimity of my thought and my indubitable wit'. They would desert Zverkov, he would sit to the side, saying nothing and feeling ashamed, and I would crush him. Then, perhaps, I would make up with him and raise a friendly glass – but the nastiest and most offensive of all was that I knew it, I knew it totally and for certain, that in reality I didn't need any of it, and that in reality, I absolutely didn't wish to crush, subjugate or fascinate them and that, should I have achieved this result entirely, then I for one wouldn't have given a fig. Oh, how I prayed to God that this day would pass the more quickly. With inexpressible sorrow, I went up to the window, opened the upper pane and peered out into the turbid gloom of thickly falling wet snow.

At last my rotten little wall clock hissed five o'clock. I grabbed my hat and, trying hard not to glance at Apollon, who had awaited the issuing of his salary ever since morning but from his own pride hadn't wanted to say anything, I crawled past him through the doorway and into a coach, which I had especially ordered with my last *poltinnik*,[25] and I rolled up like a lord to the Hôtel de Paris.

IV

I had known even the day before that I would be the first to arrive. But being first wasn't the point.

Not only was no one there but I barely managed to find our room. The table wasn't even fully laid. What did it mean? After many inquiries I finally got it out of a servant that the dinner was ordered for six o'clock and not for five. This was confirmed at the buffet, too. I was ashamed to have to ask. It was still only twenty-five minutes past five. If they had changed the hour then they should have notified me of it, at any rate; there was the municipal post for that, and they shouldn't have subjected me to such shame and . . . well, in front of the servants, at least. I sat down; the servant started to lay the table; the whole thing seemed somehow even more offensive in his presence. Towards six o'clock, they brought in candles, in addition to the lamps already burning in the room. The servant hadn't thought, however, to bring them in straight away when I arrived. In the next room two gloomy guests were dining at different tables, in silence, looking angry. There was a lot of noise coming from a distant room, shouting even, the laughter of a whole band of people and some filthy yelps in French: it was a dinner with ladies. In a word, it was nauseating. Rarely have I spent more foul moments, and such was it that when they all appeared together at exactly six o'clock, I was at first so overjoyed to see them it was as though they were some kind of liberators, and I almost forgot that I was supposed to look offended.

Zverkov walked in before the rest, evidently being the leader. He was laughing and so were the rest of them; but upon seeing me, Zverkov assumed a dignified air, approached me unhurriedly, slightly bending at the waist, as though he was flirting, and then offered me his hand, somewhat but not very affectionately, with a sort of caution, and almost with the politeness of a general, as though, in offering his hand, he were guarding himself from something. I had pictured, to the contrary, that as soon as he entered he would start laughing with his old laugh, thinly and yelpingly, and with his first word the feeble jokes and witticisms would begin. I had been preparing for them ever since the evening before but I could never have ever expected such condescending, such senior-ranking endearment. So, therefore, now he considered himself to be immeasurably above me in every respect? If he had just wanted to offend me with this general-like behaviour then it wouldn't have mattered, I thought to myself, I would have got him back somehow. But what if, in actual fact, without any desire to offend, the serious little idea had crawled into that muttonhead that he was immeasurably above me and could not look upon me in any way other than patronisingly? I was already starting to gasp from this supposition alone.

'I was surprised to learn of your desire to take part with us,' he began, lisping and sputtering and drawing out his words, which he hadn't done before. 'You and I have somehow managed to miss one another. You've been avoiding us. Without cause. We aren't as scary as we might seem to you. Well, sir, in any case, I'm glad to re-ne-ew . . .' And he casually turned to put his hat on the windowsill.

'Have you been waiting long?' Trudolyubov asked.

'I came at exactly five o'clock as I was yesterday directed,' I answered loudly and with irritation that promised an imminent explosion.

'Did you not let him know that we changed the hour?' Trudolyubov turned to Simonov.

'I didn't – forgot,' he replied, but without any regret, and then, without apologising to me, he went off to see about the *hors d'oeuvre*.

'So, you've been here an hour already – poor you!' Zverkov cried out mockingly, because, in his understanding, this really must be terribly funny. Following suit, the rascal

85

Ferfichkin burst out laughing in a ringing and rascally little way, like a little mutt. He found my situation very funny and humiliating.

'It isn't funny at all!' I cried to Ferfichkin, getting more and more irritated. 'Others are to blame, and not I. They neglected to inform me. This – this – this . . . is just absurd.'

'It's not only absurd but something else, too,' Trudolyubov muttered, naively stepping up on my behalf. 'You are too gentle. It was simply impolite. Of course, it wasn't intentional. How could Simonov . . . hmph!'

'If he had played such a trick on me,' Ferfichkin commented, 'I would—'

'But you should have asked for something to be brought to you,' Zverkov interrupted. 'Or simply have asked to dine without waiting for us to come.'

'Please allow that I could have done that without your permission,' I snapped back. 'The fact that I waited was—'

'Let us sit, gentlemen,' cried Simonov as he walked back in, 'everything is ready. I can vouch for the champagne, it is excellently chilled. You see, I didn't know your address, where does one find you?' He turned to me suddenly, but again without looking at me somehow. It was clear that he had something against me. Must have had second thoughts after yesterday.

Everyone sat down; I sat down too. The table was round. Trudolyubov settled on my left, and Simonov to the right. Zverkov sat opposite; Ferfichkin was beside him, between him and Trudolyubov.

'Te-e-ell me, are you . . . in a department?'

Zverkov continued to focus on me. Seeing that I was embarrassed, he seriously imagined that he needed to be kind to me and to cheer me up, so to speak.

What – does he want me to throw a bottle at him? I thought, in a rage. I wasn't used to this and was getting annoyed somehow unnaturally fast.

'In N— office,' I replied curtly, looking at my plate.

'And do you find it . . . p-profitable? Do-o tell what ma-ade you leave your last job?'

'What ma-a-ade me leave was that I wanted to leave my last job,' I drew the words out three times more, having already almost lost control of myself.

Ferfichkin snickered. Simonov looked at me ironically. Trudolyubov stopped eating and started to observe me with curiosity.

It grated on Zverkov but he didn't want to notice it.

'We-ell, and how is your keep?'

'Which keep?'

'That is, your salary?'

'Come now, why are you examining me?'

However, I then went on to say how much salary I receive. I turned terribly red.

'Modest,' Zverkov remarked importantly.

'Yes, sir, one musn't dine at restaurants on that!' Ferfichkin added, obnoxiously.

'In my opinion that is just poor,' Trudolyubov remarked seriously.

'And how thin you have become, how you have changed . . . since . . .' Zverkov added with a tinge of venom and a certain obnoxious pity as he surveyed me and my attire.

'You're totally embarrassing him now,' Ferfichkin cried, giggling.

'My dear sir, please know that I am not embarrassed,' I burst out at last. 'Listen! I am dining here in a "restaurant" with my own money, with my own, no one else's, take note Monsieur Ferfichkin.'

'Wha-at! Who here isn't dining with their own money? It's as if you . . .' Ferfichkin fixed onto me, turning red like a crab, and looked me in the eye with a fury.

'So-o,' I replied, feeling that I had gone too far, 'I suggest that we would be better off discussing something more intelligent.'

'You, it seems, intend to show us your intelligence?'

'Do not worry, that would be quite extraneous here.'

'Now why are you, my good sir, cackling like that, eh? Have you left your mind and gone off your rocker at your *l*epartment?'

'Enough, gentlemen, enough!' Zverkov cried out, omnipotently.

'How stupid!' Simonov muttered.

'Really, it is stupid, we have gathered together in friendly company to send off a dear friend on his voyages, and you are keeping count,' Trudolyubov began, gruffly addressing me alone. 'You imposed yourself on us yesterday, so don't upset the general harmony.'

'Enough, enough,' Zverkov cried. 'Let's stop this, gentlemen, it's not appropriate. Better that I tell you how I nearly got married two days ago . . .'

And then began some farcical story about how this gentleman almost got married two days ago. There wasn't a word about marriage, though, but the story twinkled with generals, colonels and even court dignitaries, and Zverkov seemed to be at the top of their ranks. Laughs of approval started up; Ferfichkin even yelped.

They'd all left me to one side and I sat crushed and ruined.

Good God, this can't be my milieu! I thought. And what a fool I have made of myself before them! But I've allowed Ferfichkin too much. They think, those nitwits, that they've done me an honour by giving me a seat at their table, while they don't understand that it is I – I, who have done them the honour and not they me! 'You've become thin! Your attire!' Oh, these damn trousers! Zverkov noticed the yellow stain on my knee just now. What's the point! Right now, this very minute I will stand up from the table and take up my hat and just leave, not saying a word . . . out of contempt! And tomorrow – a duel! The scoundrels. I won't bemoan the seven roubles. Perhaps they'll think . . . the devil may care! I do not bemoan the seven roubles! I am leaving this very minute!

It goes without saying that I stayed put.

I drank Lafite and sherry by the glassful in my woe. I was out of habit so I quickly became tipsy and with this tipsiness my vexation grew. I suddenly wanted to insult them all in the most impertinent way and only then take my leave. Seize the moment and show them what I'm made of – and let them say: he may be silly but he's clever . . . and . . . and . . . well, in a word, may the devil take them!

Insolently, I took them all in with my dazed eyes. But it was as though they had forgotten me completely. They were noisy, shouty, merry. Zverkov was speaking all the while. I started to listen. Zverkov was telling a story about some splendid lady whom he had led at last to a declaration of love (of course, he was lying like a horse), and that he had been helped in the matter by his intimate friend, some kind of princeling, a hussar called Kolya, who owned three thousand souls.

'But meanwhile, this Kolya who has three thousand souls,

somehow didn't come here to see you off,' I suddenly said, breaking into the conversation.

'You are drunk at this point.' Trudolyubov finally agreed to acknowledge me, contemptuously glancing in my direction. Zverkov looked me over without saying a word, as though I was a bug. I lowered my eyes. Simonov quickly started pouring the champagne.

Trudolyubov held up his glass and everyone followed suit except me.

'To your health, and a good journey to you!' he cried to Zverkov. 'To years of old, gentlemen, and to our future – hurrah!'

Everyone drank and clambered to kiss Zverkov. I didn't stir; the full glass before me stood untouched.

'Aren't you going to drink?' Trudolyubov bellowed, losing his patience and addressing himself to me threateningly.

'I want to make a speech for my own part, something special . . . and then I will drink, Mister Trudolyubov.'

'Nasty little curmudgeon!' muttered Simonov.

I straightened myself in my chair and took up my glass in a frenzy, preparing for something extraordinary though I myself didn't yet know exactly what I would say.

'*Silence!*' Ferfichkin cried out in French.[26] 'And now for something intelligent!'

Zverkov waited very seriously, understanding what was happening.

'Mister Lieutenant Zverkov,' I began, 'please know that I hate phrases, phrasemongers and tightly cinched waists. This is my first point, and the second will follow it.'

Everyone stirred vigorously.

'My second point: I hate little dalliances and their dalliancers! And especially the dalliancers!

'My third point: I love truth, sincerity and honesty,' I continued almost mechanically because I myself was freezing with horror, not able to comprehend how I could speak this way. 'I love thought, Monsieur Zverkov; I love real comraderie, on an equal footing, and not . . . hm . . . I love . . . Well, but why not? And I drink to your health, Monsieur Zverkov. Seduce the Circassian girls, shoot the enemies of the fatherland and . . . and . . . to your health, Monsieur Zverkov!'

Zverkov stood up from his chair, bowed to me and said, 'I thank you very much.' He was terribly offended and even paled.

'The devil take him,' Trudolyubov bellowed, banging the table with his fist.

'No, sir, he should get one on the chin for that!' Ferfichkin yelped.

'He should be thrown out!' Simonov muttered.

'Not a word, gentlemen, not a gesture!' Zverkov cried solemnly, stopping the general indignation. 'I thank you all but I am myself capable of showing him the price of his words!'

'Mister Ferfichkin, tomorrow you will give me satisfaction for your present words!' I said loudly, addressing myself to Ferfichkin with importance.

'You mean a duel, sir? As you please,' he replied; but I probably seemed so ridiculous in challenging him and it was so at odds with my appearance that the rest of them fell about laughing, with Ferfichkin following suit.

'Now, forget him! He's already totally drunk!' Trudolyubov said with loathing.

'I'll never forgive myself for writing his name down!' Simonov muttered again.

And now I should throw a bottle at them all, I thought, taking up a bottle and . . . I poured myself a full glass.

No, better still, I'll stay 'til the end! I continued thinking. You would be pleased, gentlemen, if I left. Not for anything. I will sit here on purpose and drink to the very end as a sign that I do not bestow you with the slightest importance. I will sit and drink, because this is a tavern, and I paid money for entrance. I will sit and drink because I consider you pawns, inconsequential pawns. I will sit and drink . . . and sing if I want to, yes, sir, and sing because I have the right . . . to sing . . . hm.

But I didn't sing. I just tried not to look at any of them; I assumed a most independent pose and waited with impatience for them to speak to me themselves *first*. But no one spoke to me. And how, how I desired at that moment to be reconciled with them! Eight o'clock struck, and nine finally, too. They moved from the table to the sofa. Zverkov spread himself over a chaise longue, putting one foot on a small round table. They brought the wine over. He did in actual fact treat them to three bottles. I was, of course, not invited. Everyone sat around him on the sofa. They were listening to him with near veneration. It was obvious that they loved him. For what? For what? I was thinking to myself. Occasionally they would come to a drunken ecstasy and embrace each other. They were speaking about the Caucasus, about the nature of true passion, about cards, about advantageous placements in the service; about how much salary was gained by Hussar Podkharzhevsky, whom none of them knew personally but they rejoiced that he earned so much; about the unusual beauty and grace of Princess D—, whom none of them had ever seen; and finally they got to the point that Shakespeare was immortal.

I smiled derisively and paced the other side of the room,

exactly across from the sofa, along the length of the wall and back. With all my strength I wanted to show them that I could make do without them; and meanwhile, I purposely stomped around with my boots, stepping down on my heels. But it was all in vain. *They* weren't paying attention. I had the patience to walk like that, right in front of them, from eight until eleven o'clock in exactly the same place, from the table to the stove and back from stove to table again. I'll walk as I like and no one can prevent me from doing it. Several times, the servant stopped to look at me after entering the room. My head was spinning from such frequent rotations; at some moments I felt I was delirious. Over the course of three hours I became soaked with sweat and dried off three times. At times my heart was pierced with the deepest, most poisonous pain of a thought: that ten, twenty, forty years would pass, and I would still, even in forty years' time, with repugnance and humiliation, remember these as the filthiest, most absurd and most terrible minutes of my whole life. It was impossible for someone to humiliate himself more unscrupulously and voluntarily, and I knew this fully – fully – but still continued to pace from the table to the stove and back again. 'Oh, if only you knew what thought and feeling I am capable of and how cultivated I am!' I thought at some points, mentally addressing the sofa where my enemies were sitting. But my enemies were behaving as though I wasn't even in the room. Once, just one time, they turned to me, it was when Zverkov started talking about Shakespeare and I suddenly laughed derisively. I snorted in such an artificial and nasty way that they all stopped their conversation abruptly and watched me in silence for about two minutes, seriously, without laughing, as I walked along the wall from the table to the stove and *paid them no attention at all*. But nothing came of it: they didn't say anything and after two minutes they abandoned me again. Eleven o'clock struck.

'Gentlemen,' cried Zverkov, getting up from the sofa, 'let's go over *there* now.'

'Of course, of course!' the others said.

I turned to Zverkov sharply. I was tormented and warped to such a degree that I would have slit my throat and ended it all! I had a fever; my hair, wet with sweat, had dried and stuck onto my forehead and temples.

'Zverkov! I beg your pardon,' I said harshly and decisively. 'Ferfichkin, yours too, and everyone's, everyone's – I have offended you all!'

'Aha! So a duel is not for you, brother!' Ferfichkin hissed venomously.

This painfully sliced into my heart.

'No, I am not afraid of duels, Ferfichkin! I am prepared to fight you tomorrow, after our reconciliation. I even insist upon it, and you cannot refuse me. I want to prove to you that I am not afraid of duels. You will fire first, and I will shoot into the air.'

'He is gratifying himself,' Simonov commented.

'He has simply gone mad!' Trudolyubov retorted.

'Allow us to pass, why are you are standing in our way! What do you require?' Zverkov responded derisively. They had all turned red; their eyes were all glistening: they had had a lot to drink.

'I am requesting your friendship, Zverkov, I offended you, but . . .'

'Offended? You . . . me? You should know, my dear sir, that you could never, not under any circumstances, offend *me*!'

'That's enough from you – be off now!' Trudolyubov clamped down. 'Let's go.'

'Olympia is mine, gentlemen, agreed?' Zverkov cried.

'We won't dispute it, won't dispute it!' they responded to him, laughing.

I stood there as though spat upon. The gang was noisily leaving the room, Trudolyubov struck up some silly song. Simonov stayed behind for the tiniest moment in order to tip the servants. I went up to him suddenly.

'Simonov! Give me six roubles!' I said resolutely and recklessly.

He looked at me in extraordinary amazement with dulled eyes. He was drunk, too.

'You're not actually going over *there* with us?'

'Yes!'

'I don't have the money!' he snapped back, laughed contemptuously and left the room.

I grabbed at his overcoat. This was a nightmare.

'Simonov! I saw that you had money, why are you refusing me? Am I a scoundrel? Beware of refusing me: if only you knew, if only you knew, why I am asking! Everything depends on this, my whole future, all my plans.'

Simonov pulled out the money and almost threw it at me.

'Take it, if you are so shameless!' he said pitilessly and ran off to catch them up.

I stayed behind for a moment alone. There was disorder, leftovers, a smashed wine glass on the floor, spilt wine, the remains of cigarettes, drunkenness and delirium in my head, tormenting sorrow in my heart, and finally, the waiter, who had seen it all and heard it all, was looking curiously into my eyes.

'I'm coming!' I cried. 'They will either fall to their knees,

hugging my knees and begging for my friendship or . . . or I
will slap Zverkov in the face!'

V

'So there it is – there it is at last – an encounter with real
life,' I muttered, running headlong down the stairs. 'This
isn't the Pope leaving Rome and setting off for Brazil
anymore; this isn't a ball at Lake Como anymore!'

You are a scoundrel, bolted through my head, if you laugh
at this now.

'So be it!' I cried, replying to myself. 'Now everything
is lost!'

Their tracks had gone cold; but it didn't matter, I knew
where they had gone.

At the steps stood a lone *vanka*, a night coachman, in
a coarse coat powdered all over with wet and warm-looking
snow that continued to fall. It was steamy and stuffy. His
small, shaggy skewbald little horse was also powdered with
snow and was coughing, too; I remember this very well. I
rushed at the hessian-covered sledge; but as soon as I had
lifted my foot to get into it, the memory of how Simonov
had just given me those six roubles blindsided me and I
flopped like a sack into the sledge.

'No! I have a lot to do in order to redeem all of this!'
I cried. 'And I will redeem it this very night or I will die on
the spot. Off we go!'

We started off. A whole whirlwind was spinning in my
head.

They won't deign to get on their knees and beg for my friendship. That is a mirage, a vulgar mirage, it's disgusting, romantic and fantastical; it's another ball on Lake Como. And that is why I *must* slap Zverkov in the face! I am obliged to do it. And so it's decided. I am rushing now to slap his face.

'Faster!'

The *vanka* began to tug at the reins.

As soon as I go in I will slap him. Should I say a few words as a sort of preface to the slap? No! I will just go in and slap. They will all be sitting in the drawing room and he will be on the sofa with Olympia. Damned Olympia! She once laughed at my physique and refused me. I will pull Olympia by the hair and Zverkov by the ears! No, better just by one ear, and I'll lead him around the room with it. They, maybe they'll all start beating me and shove me out. That is likely, even. Well, let them! I will still have first given the slap – it was my initiative – and according to the rules of honour that is everything. He is already branded and will not be able to wipe that slap from himself with blows of any kind, except in a duel. He will have to fight. So let them beat me. Let them, the ingrates! Trudolyubov will beat me especially: he is so strong; Ferfichkin will nag at me from the side and will surely go for the hair, I'd say. But let them, let them! That's why I'm going. Those muttonheads will be forced to figure out the tragedy in all this! When they drag me to the doors, I will shout at them that in fact they are not worth my little finger.

'Faster, driver, faster!' I cried to the *vanka*.

He started and flicked his whip. I had cried out savagely.

At daybreak we will fight, that is decided. I am finished with the department. Ferfichkin just now said 'lepartment' instead of 'department'. But where will I get pistols? Nonsense! I will draw my salary in advance and buy them. And the gunpowder, the bullet? That is the job of the second. But how to get it all done before daybreak? And where will I get a second? I don't have any friends.

'Nonsense!' I cried, stirring myself into even more of a frenzy. 'Nonsense!'

The first man I meet in the street, the first I greet, he is obliged to be my second – it's just like pulling a drowning man from the water. The most eccentric situations should be permitted. Even if I asked the director himself to be my second tomorrow, even he would have to consent if only from feelings of chivalry and he'd have to keep the secret, too! Anton Antonich . . .

But in fact, at that very moment, the vileness and total absurdity of my suppositions – and the flip side of the coin, too – were clearer and brighter to me than to anyone in the whole world, but . . .

'Faster, driver, faster, you scoundrel, faster!'

'Ekh, sir!' muttered nature's strongman.

The cold suddenly covered me.

Wouldn't it be better . . . wouldn't it be better . . . to go straight home? Oh, good Lord! Why, why did I summon myself to this dinner yesterday? But no, it's impossible! And three hours of pacing from table to stove? No, they, it is they – and no one else – who must pay for this pacing! They must clear this dishonour!

'Faster!'

And what if they turn me in to the police? They wouldn't dare! They'd be afraid of a scandal. And what if Zverkov refuses to the duel out of contempt? This is likely, even. But then I will show them . . . I will rush upon the posting station when he is due to leave tomorrow, and grab him by the leg, tear off his overcoat, just as he is climbing into the carriage. I will seize hold of his arm with my teeth, and I will bite him. 'So you see to what extremes you will lead a desperate man!' Let him beat me on the head, and they can come at me from behind. I will shout to the crowd, 'Look here is a young puppy who is setting off to capture Circassian girls with my spittle on his face!'

It goes without saying that after this, everything will be finished! The department will have vanished from the face of the earth. They will arrest me, they will try me, throw me out of the service, put me in jail, send me to Siberia, deport me. No matter! In fifteen years' time I shall drag my pauper self in rags after him, when they let me out of jail. I will seek him out in some provincial town. He will be married and happy. He will have a grown-up daughter. I will say, 'Look, you monster, look at my sunken cheeks and my rags! I lost everything – career, happiness, art, science, *a beloved woman*, and it's all because of you. Here are some pistols. I have come to discharge my pistol and . . . and I forgive you.' Then I will shoot into the air, and he will hear neither hide nor hair of me.

I actually started to weep, even though I knew perfectly well at that moment that all of this was taken from Silvio in Lermontov's poem 'Masquerade'. And suddenly I was horribly ashamed, ashamed to the extent that I stopped the horse, and climbed down from the sledge and stood amid the snow in the middle of the street. The *vanka* watched me with astonishment, and sighed.

What was there to do? I couldn't go there – it would be a nonsense; and I couldn't leave the matter as it was because that would make it . . . Good God! How could I leave it alone! And after such insults!

'No!' I cried out, throwing myself into the sledge once again. 'It is destined, it is fate! Onwards, onwards!'

And in my impatience I hit the driver in the neck with my fist.

'What're you doin', why you hittin' me?' the little peasant shouted out, but he then lashed his nag so hard that it began to kick out with its hind legs.

Wet snow was falling in flakes but I uncovered myself, I didn't notice it. I forgot all else, because I had resolutely decided on delivering a slap and with horror I felt that this was *now definitely* going to happen right away and *no force could stop it*. Marooned streetlamps twinkled sullenly in the snowy darkness, like torches at a funeral. Snow packed itself inside my overcoat, under my jacket, into my necktie and it melted there. I didn't cover myself up – all was lost anyway!

Finally, we had arrived. I jumped out, almost unconscious, ran up the steps and started to bang on the door with my hands and feet. My legs, especially at the knee, had weakened terribly. The door was opened quickly somehow; they must have known about my arrival. (Actually, Simonov had warned them, perhaps, that there might be another coming, because you had to warn them here and take precautions in general. This was one of the 'fashion shops' they had in those days, which were long ago destroyed by the police. In the daytime it really was a shop; but in the evening, those that had a recommendation could come as a guest.) I passed through the small dark shop with quick steps into a familiar room. Only one candle burned there, and I stopped in amazement: no one was there.

'Where are they, then?' I asked someone.

They, of course, had already managed to disperse.

In front of me stood a person with a stupid smile, the madam herself, who knew me somewhat. After a minute the door opened and another person entered.

Without paying attention to anything, I walked the length

of the room and I suppose I was talking to myself. It was as if I had been saved from death and I felt a particular joy with my whole being. Indeed, I would have slapped him, I would have invariably, invariably, slapped him! But they aren't here now . . . everything has vanished, everything has changed! I looked around. I couldn't yet gather my wits. I mechanically looked over at the girl who had walked in: before me flashed a fresh, young, somewhat pale face, with straight dark eyebrows and a serious, somewhat surprised gaze. I liked this immediately. I would have hated her if she had smiled. I started to look at her intensively and as if with effort: my thoughts had not fully gathered. There was something simple and kind in this face, but it was somehow serious to the point of strangeness. I was sure that she had been unsuccessful here because of this, and none of the fools here had noticed her. But she couldn't be called a beauty, even though she was tall, strong and well-built. She was dressed extremely simply. Something nasty bit me and I walked right up to her.

By accident I looked in the mirror. My excited face seemed repulsive to the extreme: pale, angry, mean, with shaggy hair. So what, I'm glad of it, I thought, I am specifically glad that I appear to her as repulsive: this is pleasant to me.

VI

Somewhere behind a partition, as if from some kind of strong pressure, as if someone was strangling it, a clock started to wheeze. After an unnaturally long wheeze, a thin, nasty and somehow surprisingly rapid chime followed, as if someone had suddenly jumped forward. It struck two. I awoke, even though I hadn't been sleeping, but only lying there in half-consciousness.

The room was narrow, cramped, low-ceilinged, stuffed with an enormous wardrobe and scattered with cardboard boxes, rags and all sorts of bits of clothing; it was almost totally in darkness. The stub of a candle that had been burning on the table at the end of the room had totally gone out, but sparked a little now and then. In a few minutes complete darkness would be upon us.

It didn't take long for me to come to my senses; everything instantly came back to me, at once, without effort, as if it had lain in wait for me in order to attack me again. Yes, and even in unconsciousness, there was still some kind of point that remained in my memory, something that I just couldn't forget, and my sleepy reveries circled it ponderously. But it was strange: everything that had happened to me that day seemed now to me, upon awakening, to have occurred long, long ago, as though I had lived it all long, long ago.

I had fumes in my head. It seemed as if something was floating above me and was pricking me, rousing me and disturbing me. Anguish and bile swelled in me again and they were seeking an outlet. Suddenly, I saw two open eyes next to me, curiously and sustainedly scrutinising me. The gaze was cold, apathetic, morose, as if totally alien; it was oppressive.

A morose thought arose in my brain and passed through my whole body with quite a nasty sensation, which was similar to the one you get when entering the underground, damp and musty. It was somehow unnatural that exactly now these two eyes had decided to start scrutinising me. I was also reminded that I hadn't spoken even one word to this being over the

last two hours and I absolutely hadn't considered it necessary;
I had enjoyed it even. Now, the absurd and disgusting idea of
this depravity suddenly presented itself, like a spider – it was
something which begins exactly from the place where true
love culminates, but it is without love, vulgar and shameless.
We looked at each other for a long time but she didn't lower
her eyes to mine and didn't alter her gaze, so that in the end
it was somehow terrifying to me.

'What's your name?' I asked abruptly, to conclude things
quickly.

'Liza,' she replied, almost whispering, but very ungra-
ciously somehow, and she turned her eyes away.

I said nothing.

'Today the weather . . . the snow . . . how vile!' I uttered,
almost to myself, melancholically putting my arm under my
head and looking at the ceiling. She didn't respond. This
whole thing was dreadful.

'Are you local?' I asked after a minute, almost in anger,
slightly turning my head towards her.

'No.'

'Where from?'

'From Riga,' she said reluctantly.

'German?'

'Russian.'

'Long time here?'

'Where?'

'In this house.'

'Two weeks.' She was speaking more and more abruptly.
The candle had totally gone out; I couldn't make out her face
anymore.

'Do you have a mother and father?'

'Yes. No. I do.'

'Where are they?'

'Over there . . . in Riga.'

'Who are they?'

'Just . . .'

'Just who? Who – what trade?'

'Tradesfolk.'

'Have you always lived with them?'

'Yes.'

'How old are you?'

'Twenty.'

'Why did you leave them?'

'Because.'

This meant: leave me alone, I feel wretched. We fell silent.

God knows why I hadn't left yet. I was becoming more and more wretched and anguished. The images of the day, without my willing them, began to come through into my memory in a disorderly way, somehow all by themselves. I suddenly remembered a scene I had witnessed that morning, on the street, when I anxiously trotted along to my duties.

'Today they were carrying a coffin and almost dropped it,' I suddenly uttered aloud, totally without wishing to start a conversation but just so, almost accidentally.

'A coffin?'

'Yes, on Sennaya Square. They were bringing it out of a basement.'

'From a basement?'

'Not from a basement but from the basement level . . . well, you know, from below . . . from a house of ill repute. There was mud everywhere. Eggshells, rubbish . . . it stank; it was foul.'

Silence.

'It's an awful day for a funeral!' I began again, just in order not to remain silent.

'How is it awful?'

'Snow, the wet . . .'

I yawned.

'Doesn't matter,' she said suddenly after a certain silence.

'No, it's vile.' I yawned again. 'The gravediggers were probably cursing because the snow soaked them. And, I suppose, there was water in the grave.'

'Why would there be water in the grave?' she asked, with a certain curiosity, but speaking out more roughly and abruptly than before.

Something suddenly started to egg me on.

'Come now, the water at the bottom must have been some six *vershok* deep. There's not one grave at Volkovo that you could dig dry.'

'Why?'

'What do you mean why? It's a watery place. There's swamp everywhere here. So they put them into the water. I've seen it myself, many times.' (I hadn't seen it even once and have never been to Volkovo, have only heard people describe it.) 'So it doesn't bother you, the idea of death?'

'Well, why should I die?' she answered, as though defending herself.

'You'll die sometime of course, and you'll die exactly like the deceased today. It was . . . also a girl. She died of consumption.'

'A wench would have died in hospital.'

She already knows about this, I thought, she said 'wench' and not 'girl'.

'She owed her madam,' I retorted, more and more egged on by the discussion. 'And she served her almost to the very end, even though she had consumption. Some cab drivers were standing around talking with the soldiers about it. They were probably her former acquaintances. They were laughing. They were planning on meeting in the tavern in her memory.' (Now, I was lying a lot.)

Silence, deep silence. She didn't even stir.

'Is it better to die in a hospital, do you think?'

'Isn't it all the same? What am I to die of, anyway?' she added, irritatedly.

'If not now then later.'

'So, later then . . .'

'If only! You're young now, good-looking, fresh – that's why they ask such a good price for you. But after a year of this life you won't be like this, you'll wither.'

'In a year?'

'In any case, in a year you'll be less valuable,' I continued, with malicious pleasure. 'You will move from here to somewhere lower, to another house. And after another year to a third house, lower and lower, and after about seven years you'll be in a basement in Sennaya Square. And that's not the worst. Worse would be if, apart from all that, you got some sort of disease, well, like a weakness in the chest . . . or you caught cold or something. Disease is hard to usher out of a life like yours. It can fasten on and then you might not be able to unfasten it. And so you die.'

'So I'll die,' she replied, totally spitefully now, and stirred quickly.

'It's a pity.'

'For whom?'

'A pity for life.'

Silence.

'Do you have a fiancé? Eh?'

'Why do you ask?'

'Oh, I'm not interrogating you. It's nothing to me. Why are you angry? You, of course, may have your troubles. What is it to me? Just a pity.'

'For whom?'

'Pity for you.'

'Not at all,' she whispered, barely audibly, and again stirred.

This immediately made me furious. What! I was so mild with her but she . . .

'Well, what do you think? On a good path are you, eh?'

'I don't think anything.'

'That's the problem – that you don't think. Realise, while there's still time. And there is still time. You are young, good-looking; you could love someone, get married, be happy.'

'Not all married women are happy,' she cut in, with the same rough patter as before.

'Not all, of course, but it would still be a lot better than being here. Far better. For if there is love, you can live without happiness. And life is good even in woe – it is good to live in this world, however you may live. But what is there here apart from . . . filth. Phooy!'

I turned away with loathing; I was no longer coldly moralising. I had myself started to feel what I was saying and was heating up. I was already thirsting to set forth the cherished little ideas that I had lived out in my corner. Something suddenly ignited me, a goal of some kind had appeared.

'Now, don't you mind that I am here – I'm not an example for you. I am maybe even worse than you. But, I came here drunk,' I said, hurrying to justify myself.

'And furthermore, men are no example for women. It's

a different business. I might defile and foul myself but I am not anyone's slave for it. I come here and I'm off again. I shake it off myself and I'm not that man anymore. But let's acknowledge that you from the very beginning are a slave. Yes, a slave! You give everything away, all of your volition. And afterwards when you want to break these chains, you can't: you will be more and more tightly enmeshed. That's what a cursed chain it is. I know it. I'm not going to talk about other things, you probably won't get it, but tell me: I suppose you already owe your madam?

'So, you see!' I added, even though she hadn't replied to me but only sat in silence, listening with her whole being. 'There's chains for you! You won't ever buy yourself out of it. That's how they do it. Same as selling your soul to the devil.

'And, moreover, I . . . Maybe I am just as unhappy, too, how would you know? And I crawled into this filth on purpose, also out of melancholy. Indeed, people drink out of woe: well, and here I am – out of woe. But tell me, what good is there in this, here; you and I have come together . . . just now, and we didn't utter a word to each other, and afterwards you started to scrutinise me like a savage and I you, also. Is that any way to love? Is that any way for a person to come together with another person? It's an outrage, that's what it is!'

'Yes!' she assented abruptly and hurriedly.

I was surprised by the hurry of this 'yes'. Did that mean she also had, maybe, the same thought wandering in her head, as she was scrutinising me just now? That means that she is actually capable of certain thoughts? Damn it, this is curious; this is *kinship*, I thought, almost rubbing my hands. But how could you come to terms with such a young soul?

It was the game of this that fascinated me most of all.

She turned her head closer to me and, it seemed to me in

the darkness, she propped it up with her hand. Maybe she was scrutinising me. How I regretted that I couldn't make out her eyes. I heard her deep breathing.

'Why did you come here?' I began, with a certain authority.

'Because.'

'But how nice to live in your father's house! Warm, so free. Your own nest.'

'And what if it's worse?'

The thought flashed in my mind that I must alight upon the right tone: sentimentality, perhaps, might not get me far.

However, that only flashed through my mind. I swear she did actually interest me. I was somehow relaxed and susceptible. And trickery goes together so well with feeling.

'Who can say!' I hurried to answer. 'All manner of things happen. Now, I'm convinced that someone has insulted you and that *others* are to blame sooner than you. Indeed, I know nothing of your story, but a girl like you probably didn't land here out of your own desire.'

'And what kind of girl am I?' she whispered. It was hardly audible but I heard it.

Damn it, I'm flattering her. That was vile. Or maybe, it was good.

She said nothing.

'Well, Liza, I will speak for myself! Had I had a family from childhood, I wouldn't be as I am today. I think about this often. Indeed, no matter how bad a family it may have been, there would still have been a father and a mother, rather than enemies, strangers. Even if they only show you love once a year. You still know that you are at home. And I grew up without a family; that's why, probably, I turned out like this . . . feelingless.'

I waited again.

Perhaps she doesn't understand, I thought, and it's silly, this moralising.

'If I were a father and I had my own daughter, I would, it seems, love a daughter more than a son, really,' I started, obliquely, as though on to something else, to distract her. I will admit, I blushed.

'Why is that?' she asked.

Ah, therefore she is listening!

'Well. I don't know, Liza. You see, I knew one father who was a strict and austere man but before his daughter he would get down on his knees, kiss her hand and foot, couldn't admire her enough, really. She danced at parties and he stood five hours in one place, not taking his eyes off her. He was mad about her; I can understand it. She would tire at night, fall asleep, and he would wake up and go to her as she slept and kiss her and make the sign of the cross over her. He walked around in a dirty frock coat, he was stingy with everyone, but he'd spend his very last on her, give her expensive gifts, and he was overjoyed if she was pleased with his gifts. A father always loves daughters more than the mother does. Living at home is a joy to some girls! But, I suppose, I would never let my own daughter get married.'

'Really, how is that?' she asked, almost smirking.

'I would be jealous, God knows. Well, how could she kiss anyone else? To love a stranger more than a father? It is dreadful to imagine it. Of course, this is all nonsense. Of course, everyone is reasonable in the end. But, I think, before giving her away, I would be tormented by nothing but worries: I would reject her suitors again and again. And it would all end anyway with me giving her to the one that she herself loves. Indeed the one that the daughter herself loves is always the one that seems the worst of all to the father. That's how it is. Many troubles arise in families because of this.'

'And others are happy to sell their daughters, rather than giving them into marriage honourably,' she said suddenly.

Ah! This was it!

'This, Liza, happens in those accursed families where there is neither God nor love,' I picked up with fervour, 'and where there is no love, there is no reason. There are such families, in truth, but I'm not talking about them. You, it's evident, didn't see kindness in your own family since you speak thus. What a genuinely unhappy girl you are. Hm . . . Such things happen mostly because of poverty.'

'So it's better among the gentry, then? Honest people live nicely, even in poverty.'

'Hm . . . yes. Maybe. But there's another thing, Liza: man loves only to count his woes, and never counts his happinesses. But if he counted them as he should then he would see that there is enough of each reserved for him. Well, and what if everything goes well for the family, God blesses it, the husband turns out to be good, loves you, cherishes you, doesn't leave you! Good to be in that family! Even when it's sometimes mixed with grief, it's good; is there anywhere, after all, where woe is absent? You will, maybe, get married, and then *you'll see for yourself*. And, at least in the very first part of marriage to the one you love, there is happiness, how much happiness sometimes! It's nearly always that way. In the early days even arguments with your husband end well. Some women, the more they cook up fights, the more they love it. Really, I knew one just like that. "Right, so, I love you," she'd say, "very much, and it is out of love that I torment you, so feel it." Do you know that a person can purposefully torment another out of love? It's women mostly. She thinks to herself,

since I will go on to love him so much, to give him such
affection, it isn't a sin now to torment him a bit. And everyone
in the household rejoices in you, and it is good, and merry,
and calm, and honest . . . And then there are others, jealous
ones – I knew one like this. The husband goes out somewhere
and she can't bear it, so that very night she jumps up and
runs off secretly to see: is he there, is he in that house, is he
with her? This is bad. And she knows it herself that it's bad,
and her heart sinks and she blames herself, but she loves him;
it's all from love. And how good it is to make peace after a
fight, to recognise her errors or to forgive him! And how good
it is for both, how good it suddenly becomes, just as if they
were first meeting again, marrying again; love begins anew
between them. And no one, no one should know what happens
between a husband and wife if they love each other. And
whatever quarrels emerge between them, they shouldn't even
call on their own mothers to judge it or tell things about each
other to others. They themselves are the judges. Love is a
divine mystery and it should be closed from the eyes of all
others, whatever happens in it. It is more sacred this way, and
better. They respect each other more and much is based on
respect. And if there was once love, if they married in love
then why should love pass? Should it not be sustained? It's a
rare incidence when it can't be sustained. Well, and if the
husband is a kind and honest man, then how can love pass?
The initial love of marriage will pass, it's true, but then an
even better love comes along. Then they unite in soul, all
their dealings become common dealings; there won't be any
secrets from each other. And children will come, and then
even the most difficult of times will seem happy, as long as
they love and are brave. Then even work is a joy; then even
when you sometimes forego bread for the sake of your children

it will also be a joy. Indeed, they will love you for it afterwards; you are, that means, accumulating. The children grow, and you feel that you are an example to them, that you are their support; that you will die and they will carry your feelings and thoughts on themselves, since they received them from you; they will take on your image and likeness. And so, it is a great duty. How could a father and a mother not unite in this? They say, rightly, that having children is hard. Who says this? It is a heavenly happiness! Do you like little children, Liza? I like them awfully. You know, when a little pink baby boy suckles at your breast, which husband's heart doesn't turn towards his wife when looking upon her sitting there with his child? The little baby is pink, chubby, it sprawls out, luxuriates; juicy little hands and little feet, clean little nails, tiny, so tiny, that it's funny to look at them, and little eyes which seem to understand everything. And he suckles, tugging at your breast with his little hand, playing. Father comes up and the baby tears away from the breast, throwing himself backwards, looking at his father, and laughs as though it were God knows how funny and again, again takes to suckling. Or else he will take it and he will bite his mother's breast if his little teeth are coming through, and then with his little eyes he will look at her from the side. "You see, I bit you!" Yes, is that not a happiness when the three of them, husband, wife and child, are together? Much can be forgiven for the sake of such moments. No, Liza, one must first learn oneself how to live, and only then blame others!'

It's imagery, it's a bit of imagery that I need! So I thought to myself, even though, God knows, I was speaking with feeling. I suddenly blushed. And what if she bursts into laughter, where will I hide then? This idea brought me into a panic. Towards the end of that speech I had become actually impassioned, and now my vanity was suffering in some way. Silence continued. I wanted to nudge her, even.

'You're a bit . . .' she began suddenly, and stopped.

But now I understood everything: in her voice something else was quivering, it wasn't sharp, it wasn't rough and unyielding as it had been but somewhat soft and bashful, and so bashful that I suddenly became ashamed myself, felt guilty before her.

'What?' I asked with tender curiosity.

'Well, you . . .'

'What?'

'You are somehow . . . exactly like in books,' she said and it was as if suddenly there was again something mocking to be heard in her voice.

This remark stung me painfully. I hadn't expected it.

I did not understand that she was purposefully masking herself with this mockery, that this was the usual ruse of bashful and chaste-hearted people, when one roughly and importunately pokes one nose into their souls – they won't yield, out of pride, until the last moment, and they are afraid to express feelings before you. I should have guessed it, given the timidity with which she advanced her mockery, with several attempts, only eventually resolving to articulate it. But I didn't guess it and an evil feeling encompassed me.

Just you wait, I thought.

VII

'Eh, enough, Liza, what do books have to do with it when it's just revulsion on your behalf? Well, not just on your behalf.

All this has now awoken in my soul . . . Can it be, can it be that you don't find it repulsive here? No, it's clear that habit counts for a lot! The devil knows what habit will make of a person. Can you seriously think that you will never get old, that you will be eternally good-looking and that they will keep you here for evermore? Never mind the mischief of this place. Now, here's what I'll tell you about that, about your current life: here you are, you're at least young, comely, good-looking, you have soul, you have feeling. Well, then, and do you know that the moment I woke up just now I was instantly repulsed, being here with you! Only in a drunken state can one land here. But if you were in another place, living like good people live, then it might be that I wouldn't just court you but would simply fall in love with you, I would be glad of a glance from you, not to mention a word. I would stand and wait for you at the gate; I would stand on my knees before you as long as needed; I would look upon you as my future bride and would consider it an honour so to do. I wouldn't dare to think anything impure about you. But here, I know that all I need do is whistle and whether you want to or not you will follow me, and I do not respect your will but you do mine. Even the lowliest *muzhik* gets himself hired as a labourer but he still doesn't enslave himself totally – and also, he knows that there's a time limit to it. But where is your time limit? Just think: what are you giving away here? What are you enslaving? Your soul, your soul, over which you are powerless, you are enslaving it together with your body! You give your love in desecration to every drunkard! Love! But this love – it is everything, it is a diamond, a maiden's treasure! Indeed, in order to deserve this love, another man would be prepared to lay down his soul and go to his death. But what is your love now worth? You've been bought totally, your whole self, so why strive for love here when anything is possible even without love. And there isn't really a greater insult for a girl, don't you understand? Yes, I've heard that they humour you, you fools, and let you have lovers. Oh, indeed that is a treat – a lie, a laugh at your expense, and you believe it. Does he, in actual fact, really love you, this lover? I don't believe it. How can he love you when he knows that you can be summoned away from him at any minute? He would be scum, if so! Do you think he respects you one jot? What do you have in common with him? He is laughing at you and he is robbing you, too – that's all there is to his love! Good that he doesn't beat you. Maybe he does beat you. Go ahead and ask him, if you have one like him: will he marry you? Well, he'll laugh in your face, if he doesn't spit in it or hit it; while he himself is maybe only worth two broken *grosh*[27] in all. And for what, one wonders, have you spoiled your life? Because they pour you coffee and feed you well? But why are they feeding you? Another girl, an honest one, wouldn't be able to take a crumb into her mouth because she'd know why they were feeding her. You have debts here, and you will continue to be in debt here, and to the very last you will be in debt here, until such a time as the guests start to be squeamish about you. And this will soon happen, don't rely upon your youth. Here, all of that flies off post-haste. They'll throw you out. Yes, and they won't just throw you out but, long beforehand, they'll start to carp at you, start to reproach you, to scold you. It won't be as though you hadn't given the madam your health, and spoiled your youth and soul for her for free, but as though you yourself brought ruin to her, emptied her coffers, robbed her. And don't expect any support: those other girlfriends of yours will also gun for you, in order to worm into her favour, because everyone here is in slavery, they long ago lost their conscience and compassion. They have turned so despicable that there would be nothing on earth more nasty, more mean, more insulting than their abuses. You are giving up everything down here, everything, the whole host – your health, your youth, your beauty, your hopes – and at twenty-two years of age you will look like a thirty-five-year-old, and it will be good if you aren't sick by then, pray to God for that. Indeed, right now, I dare say, you think that you have no work to do, that it's a bit of idling! But a tougher and more punitive labour has never existed in the world. The heart alone, it would seem, could cry itself out. And you won't dare say a word, not half a word, when they chase you out of here – you will go off like a culprit. You'll go on to work in another place, and then a third, and then somewhere else, even, and you'll make it to Sennaya Square in the end. And there they'll start beating you, just in passing; that's the local courtesy; there, a visitor isn't able to show you any kindness without beating you up first. You don't believe it's as nasty as that? Go on, have a look sometime and maybe you'll see it with your own eyes. I once saw a girl there on New Year's Day, standing by a door. Her people had thrown her out as a tease, to cool her off a bit because she had been howling away, and they shut the door behind her. At nine o'clock in the morning she was already totally drunk, dishevelled, half-naked, completely beaten up. Her face was powder-whitened, but she had black eyes; there was blood flowing from her teeth and nose: some coach driver had just laid into her. She was sitting on the stone stairs and in her hands was some kind of salted fish; she was howling, lamenting her 'horr-r' while she pounded the steps with her fish. And coach drivers and drunken soldiers were crowded on the porch, taunting her. You don't believe that you will be like her? I wouldn't want to believe it, either, but how do you know – maybe about eight, ten years ago she herself, with her salted fish, arrived here from somewhere; a fresh thing, like a little cherub, innocent and clean – she won't have known evil and will have blushed at every word. Maybe she was just exactly like you are: proud, easily insulted, unlike the others, someone who looked like a queen and knew that total happiness awaited the man who would love her and whom she would love. Do you see how it finished? And what if, at that very minute when she was pounding the dirty steps with her fish, drunk and dishevelled, what if at that minute, she was reminded of her past, the clean years in her father's house when she was still walking back and forth to school and the boy next door waited for her at the gate to convince her that he would love her his whole life, that he would lay down his fate for her; when they forever vowed to love one another and said they would marry as soon as they grew bigger! No, Liza, it would be a happiness, a happiness for you if somewhere, in some corner in a basement, like that woman, you quickly died of consumption. In a hospital, you say? Good, if they'll take you there, but what if the madam needs you still? Consumption is one of those diseases – it's not a fever. A person with it keeps up hope and says that they are well until the last minute. You reassure yourself. And this benefits the madam. Don't worry, that's how it goes: you've sold your soul and furthermore you're in debt, which means you won't dare let out a squeak. And when you die everyone will abandon you, turn their backs – because what is to be got out of you then? And then they will reproach you, that you're taking up space uselessly, since you aren't dying quick enough. You won't get a drink of water easily, and it will be given with curses. They'll say, "when will you, you slut, drop dead? You're interfering with our sleep with your moans, and you're making our guests squeamish." And it's true; I have heard such words myself. They will shove you, perishing, into the most stinking corner of the basement, the dark, the damp. What then, as you lie there alone, will you be thinking about? You will die, strangers' hands will hurriedly lay you out, grumbling with impatience – no one will bless you, no one will sigh for you, and the sooner they offload you the better. They will buy a coffin, carry you out like they carried out that one today, poor thing, and will drink to your memory in the tavern. There will be sleet, scum, wet snow in your grave – no need to stand on ceremony for you. "Let her down, Vanyukha, look at the 'horr-r' – even here she has her legs up in the air, such as she was. Shorten the cords, you little imp." "It's fine as it is." "What do you mean, fine? She's on her side. She's a person all the same, or no? Okay, fine, cover her up." And they won't want to argue over you for long. They will quickly cover you up with wet, dark-blue clay and then go off to the tavern. And that will be the end of your memory on earth. Children will visit the graves of others – fathers, husbands, too – but not a tear, not a sigh, not a remembrance for you, and no one, no one, in the whole world will ever come to you; your name will disappear from the face of the earth – just as if you had never existed or been born! There will only be filth and swamp, and at night, when the dead arise, it won't matter how hard you knock on your coffin's lid. "Let me out good people, to live in the world! I lived but didn't see a life, my life was rubbed out; it was drunk away in a tavern in Sennaya Square; let me out, good people, to live once again in the world!'"

I had entered into such zeal that I began to have a spasm in my throat and I suddenly stopped, sat half up in fright and leaned my head over timorously and started to listen, my heart beating. There was good reason to be confused.

I had already long felt that I was upturning her whole soul and was shattering her heart, and the more I was convinced of this, the more I desired to attain my goal as quickly and as powerfully as possible. The game, the game had fascinated me; however, it wasn't just the game.

I knew that I was speaking stiffly, artificially, even bookishly; and, in a word, I couldn't do otherwise than to speak 'just like a book'. But this didn't trouble me. I knew, I had felt, that I'd be understood and that this bookishness might even help matters. But now, having attained this effect, I suddenly turned coward. Never, no, never, have I been witness to such despair! She was lying face downwards, forcefully pushing her face into the pillow and clutching it with both hands. Her breast was splitting. Her whole young body was shuddering as though in convulsions. Constricted sobs were confined to her breast and they tore her apart, until suddenly cries and wails burst forth. Then she pressed herself even harder into the pillow: she didn't want anyone here, not even one living soul, to know about her anguish and her tears. She was biting the pillow and bit her own hand until it bled (I saw this afterwards) or, hooking her fingers into her loosened plaits, she would stiffen with effort, holding her breath and clenching her teeth. I began to say something to her, to beg her to calm down, but I felt I didn't dare and suddenly, shivering all over, almost in horror, I took to groping around, hurriedly, however I could, gathering myself to leave. It was dark: no matter how I tried, I couldn't do it quickly. I felt a box of matches and a candlestick with a whole, unburnt candle in it. As soon as the light illuminated the room, Liza jumped up to sitting and with a kind of distorted face, with a half-mad smile, she looked at me, almost inanely. I sat down next to her and took her hands. She came to her senses, threw herself toward me, wanted to embrace me but didn't dare and quietly bowed her head before me.

'Liza, my friend, I shouldn't have . . . Forgive me,' I started. But she squeezed my hands in her fingers with such strength that I guessed that I was saying the wrong thing and stopped.

'Here is my address, Liza, come to me.'

'I will come,' she whispered resolutely, still not lifting her head.

'So, I am going now, farewell . . . until we meet again.'

I stood up, and she stood up and suddenly went totally red, shuddered, grabbed the kerchief that was lying on a chair and threw it around her shoulders up to her very chin. Having done this, she smiled again somewhat abnormally, and blushed, and looked at me strangely. It pained me; I hurried to leave, to vanish.

'Wait,' she said suddenly, when I was already in the hall right by the doors, stopping me with her hand on my overcoat. She put down the candle hastily and ran off – it was clear that she had remembered something or wanted to show me something. As she ran she had flushed red, her eyes were sparkling and a smile had appeared on her lips – what could it be? I waited for her against my will; she made her return after a minute, with a gaze as if she were asking forgiveness for something. Altogether it was not any more the same face, the same gaze as it had been: morose, mistrustful and obstinate. Her gaze now was imploring, soft, and also trusting, affectionate, timid. The same look that children have when they look at people they very much love, when they are asking for something. Her eyes were light-brown, beautiful eyes – lively, capable of expressing love but also morose hatred.

She proffered me a piece of paper without explaining

anything to me, as if I were some higher being and should have known without any explanation. Her whole face beamed at that moment, with the most naive, almost childlike triumph. I unfolded the paper. It was a letter to her from a medical student or something of the sort – a very high-flown, florid but extremely respectable declaration of love. I don't quite remember now how it was expressed, but I recall very well that through the sublime syllables you could see true feeling, which it isn't possible to fake. When I had finished reading I met her hot, curious and childishly impatient gaze. She had fastened her eyes on my face and was waiting with impatience – what would I say? In a few words, hurriedly, but somehow joyfully and as though she were proud of it, she explained to me that she was at some kind of dance, in a family house, the guest of some 'very very good people, *family people* and where *they know nothing*, absolutely nothing about . . .' because she only came here just recently and only because . . . and she hasn't at all decided whether to stay and was certainly going to leave as soon as she had paid her debt. Well, and there was this student there who danced and talked with her the whole evening, and it turned out that he knew her back in Riga, back when she was a child and they had played together, but it was a very long time ago, and he knows her parents but *about this* he knew nothing – nothing – nothing at all and didn't suspect anything! And then the next day after the dance (three days ago) he had sent this letter through the friend with whom she had come to the party . . . and . . . well, that was it.

She ashamedly lowered her sparkling eyes when she had finished her account.

The poor thing, she had kept this student's letter like a jewel and had run to get this, her only jewel, not wishing me to leave without knowing that she is loved honestly and sincerely, that some speak to her with respect. This letter was probably fated to lie in a box without further consequence. But it didn't matter; I was sure that she would keep it her whole life, like a jewel, as her pride and her justification, and just now she had remembered it and brought this letter to me so that she could naively take pride in herself before me, resurrect herself in my eyes, so that I would also see it, and I would also praise her. I didn't say anything, shook her hand and left. I wanted to leave so much. I went the whole way home on foot, despite the fact that wet snow continued to fall in big flakes. I was spent, crushed, bewildered. But the truth was already flashing through my bewilderment. A foul truth!

VIII

However, I didn't swiftly agree to recognise this truth. Having woken up in the morning after several hours of deep, leaden sleep and immediately grasping the whole of yesterday's events, I was amazed at my *sentimentality* with Liza, at all 'yesterday's horrors and pities'. What a stupid bit of womanish hysteria, phoo! I decided. And why did I foist my address on her? And what if she comes? Fine, then, let her come; what does it matter. But it's *obvious* that the main and most important matter was now not this: I had to hurry and, whatever it took, I needed to save my reputation in the eyes of Zverkov and Simonov. This was the main matter. I totally forgot about Liza for the rest of the morning, having busied myself with it.

First of all I had to immediately repay my debt to Simonov. I resorted to desperate measures: borrowing fifteen roubles from Anton Antonovich. As fate would have it he was in a most excellent mood that morning and gave it to me right then, at my first request. I was very glad that, having signed the receipt with a kind of jaunty gesture, I *casually* informed him that yesterday 'I caroused with some friends at the Hôtel de Paris. We were sending off a comrade, a childhood friend you might even say, and, you know, he was a big carouser, a spoilt one – well, and it goes without saying, he's from a good family, has considerable means, a sparkling career, he's witty, genteel, carries on intrigues with certain ladies, if you know what I mean. We drank an extra "half-dozen" and . . .' And that was it. It was all uttered very lightly, familiarly and smugly.

Arriving home, I quickly wrote to Simonov.

To this moment I am in admiration, recalling the truly gentlemanly, genial, sincere tone of my letter. I blamed myself for everything deftly and nobly, but, most importantly, entirely without a spare word. I tried to excuse myself, 'if I might be allowed to try to excuse myself', with the fact that, completely unused to drinking wine, I had become drunk at the first glass, which allegedly I drank before they arrived, when I was waiting for them at the Hôtel de Paris between five and six o'clock. I asked for Simonov's pardon, principally; and I asked him then to relay my excuses to all the others, especially to Zverkov, whom it seems I insulted 'as I recall, as though in a dream'. I added that I would myself have gone to each of them, but my head hurt, and more than anything, I was ashamed. I was especially pleased with 'a certain lightness', even almost an off-handedness (but thoroughly polite), which had suddenly affected my quill and instantly gave them to understand, better than any possible argument, that I looked upon 'all of yesterday's muck' rather independently. I was altogether entirely not killed on the spot, as you, sirs, probably think, but to the contrary, I look upon it just as I should look upon it, as a calmly self-respecting gentleman. A good man is beyond reproach, so to speak.

Might there even be a kind of baronial playfulness to it? I admired the note, reading it again. And all because I am a cultivated and educated man! Others in my place would not have known how to disentangle themselves, but here I am, extricated and carousing once again, and all because I am 'an educated and cultivated man of our times'. Indeed, perhaps it was all due to yesterday's wine. Hm. Well, no, it wasn't from the wine. And I didn't drink any vodka from five to six o'clock when I was waiting for them. I had lied to Simonov; I had lied shamelessly; and I'm still not ashamed.

I couldn't give a fig though! The main thing was that I was rid of it.

I put six roubles in the letter, sealed it and prevailed upon Apollon to take it to Simonov. Having learnt that there was money in the letter, Apollon became more respectful and agreed to go. Towards the evening, I went out for a stroll. My head was still hurting and spinning after yesterday. But the more the evening wore on and the twilight grew denser, the more my impressions changed and became confused, and my thoughts followed suit. Something wouldn't die inside me, it didn't want to die in the depths of my heart and conscience, and it announced itself as burning anguish. I pushed my way through the most peopled, mercantile streets, Meshchanskaya, Sadovaya, Yusupov's Garden. I especially loved always to amble along these streets at twilight, just when the crowds thicken with all the various merchants and traders, their faces anxious to the point of fury, dispersing to their houses from their daily commission. It was exactly this cheap bustle that I liked, this impudent prosaicness. But this time the crush of the street just added to my irritation. I couldn't in any way get the better of myself, couldn't find my limits. Something was rising, rising in my soul incessantly, painfully, and it didn't want to calm down. Completely distraught, I went back home. It was exactly as if some kind of crime was pressing on my soul.

The thought that Liza might come over tormented me constantly. What was odd to me was that of all yesterday's memories, the memory of her, somehow especially, somehow completely separately, tormented me. I had already managed to forget the rest of it by evening, I'd shrugged it off and remained perfectly content with my letter to Simonov. But I was somehow not content about this. It was just as if I were tormented by Liza alone. And what if she does come? I thought, constantly. Well, so what, doesn't matter, let her come. Hm. The only awful thing is that she would see, for example, how I live. Yesterday I seemed to her like a hero . . . and now, hm! It is, however, awful that I have let myself go like this. It's just poverty in the apartment. And I made up my mind yesterday to go to dinner in such an outfit! And my oilcloth sofa with its stuffing sticking out! And my dressing gown, which doesn't close! What tatters. And she will see all of it; and she will see Apollon. The swine will probably insult her. He will pick on her just to do me a discourtesy. And, of course, as is my habit, I will turn coward, will start to mince around before her, to cover myself with the flaps of my dressing gown, will start to smile, will start to lie. Oh, the awfulness! And that isn't the most significant awfulness of it all! There's something even more significant, more vile, more despicable. Yes, more despicable! And again, again I must put on this dishonest, lying mask!

Having reached this thought, I just ignited. Why dishonest? How is it dishonest? I was speaking sincerely yesterday. I remember that there was real feeling in me, also. I specifically wanted to awaken noble feeling in her . . . if she wept then that is a good thing, it will have been beneficial for her . . .

But all the same, I couldn't calm down at all.

The whole evening, when I had already returned home, when it was already past nine o'clock and according to my estimations, there was no way Liza could come, she haunted me all the same, and, above all, I remembered her in one and the same situation. Specifically, there was one moment in the whole of yesterday that especially brightly presented itself: it was when I illuminated the room with a match and saw her pale, distorted face with its martyr-like gaze. And what a piteous, what an unnatural, what a distorted smile she wore at that moment! But I didn't know then that even after fifteen years I would still imagine Liza exactly like that, with the piteous, distorted, unnecessary smile, which she wore at that minute.

The next day I was again prepared to consider it all as nonsense, frazzled nerves and above all *exaggeration*. I was always conscious of this little weak spot and sometimes I have been very much afraid of it. 'I exaggerate everything, and that's what makes me lame,' I repeated this to myself hourly. But, 'however, Liza will probably come anyway' – that was the refrain that concluded all my reasonings. I was upset to such a point that sometimes I brought myself into a rage. 'She will come! She will definitely come!' I cried, running around the room. 'If not today, then tomorrow, she will track me down! Such is the damned romanticism of all *pure hearts* like her! Oh, the abomination, oh, the silliness, oh, the narrow-mindedness of these "befouled, sentimental souls"!

Well, how can she not understand, it's as though she doesn't understand, how is that?' But that's where I'd stop myself, in great confusion.

And how few, I thought in passing, how few words were needed, how little idyll was needed (and an artificial, bookish, fabricated idyll at that) in order immediately to turn the whole of a human soul to one's own purposes! That's virginity! That's the freshness of the soil!

Sometimes the thought came to me of going myself to see her, 'to tell her everything' and to beg her not to visit me. But then, at that thought, such malice rose inside me that, it seems, I might have suddenly crushed that 'damned' Liza if she had happened to be near me, and I would have insulted her, spat at her, chased her out and struck her!

A day, however, passed, and another and a third and she didn't come, and I started to calm down. I especially cheered up and was enlivened after nine o'clock, and sometimes even started to daydream, and rather sweetly, too. So, I could save Liza, precisely because she starts to visit me and I talk to her. I develop her, I educate her. In the end, I notice that she loves me, she loves me passionately. I pretend that I don't understand. (I don't know, however, why I would pretend; just because, for aesthetics, probably.) In the end she is embarrassed, beautiful, trembling and sobbing, and throws herself at my feet and says that I am her saviour, that she loves me more than anything on earth. I am astounded; 'but, Liza,' I say, 'can you possibly think that I haven't noticed your love? I saw it all, I guessed it all, but I didn't dare to infringe upon your heart first, because you are so influenced by me and I feared that you, out of gratitude, would purposefully force yourself to respond to my love, that you would summon feelings in yourself, forcibly, which perhaps weren't there and

I didn't want that because that is . . . despotism. That is indelicate.' (Well, in a word, I blathered on with some kind of European, George Sand-ish and indescribably noble subtleties.) 'But now, now – you are mine, you are my creation, you are pure, lovely, you are my lovely wife. "*And into my house bold and free, As mistress of all, you shall be*".'28

Then we begin to live happily ever after, we travel abroad and, etc., etc. In a word, it was all becoming despicable to me, and I finished by sticking out my tongue at myself.

They won't even let her out, 'the slut'! I thought. It seems that they don't let them go out much, above all in the evenings. (For some reason it seemed inevitable to me that she would come in the evening and at seven o'clock exactly.) But she said that she hadn't become totally enslaved there, that she had her special rights – so that means . . . hm! Devil take it – she will come, she will certainly come!

It was good that Apollon distracted me at this time with his vulgarities. He drove me to the end of my patience! This was my ulcer, my scourge, sent to me by Providence. We had been constantly squabbling for several years and I hated him. My God, how I hated him! I haven't hated anybody in my whole life, it seems, as much as I hated him, especially at certain moments. He was elderly, pompous and worked partly as a tailor. I didn't know why but he despised me, beyond all measure even, and looked upon me with intolerable haughtiness. However, he looked upon everyone with haughtiness. Just a glance at his tow-haired, smoothly combed head; at the quiff that he whipped up over his forehead and greased with sunflower oil; at his solid mouth, always pulled into the form of the letter V, and you would feel straight away that before you is a being who has never doubted in himself. This was a pedant of the highest degree, the most enormous pedant of all those I had ever met on this earth; and with it, a vanity that would only befit Alexander the Great. He was in love with his every button, with each of his fingernails – absolutely in love, and he looked it, too! His attitude towards me was totally despotic, he spoke with me extremely little, and if it happened that he glanced at me then he looked at me with a hard, majestically self-confident and constantly mocking gaze, driving me sometimes into a rage. He performed his duties with such an air, as if he were doing me the greatest favour. However, he did almost exactly nothing for me and didn't consider himself at all obliged to do anything. There could be no doubt that he considered me to be the greatest of all fools in the world and if he 'retained me' then it was only just in order to receive his salary from me each month. He agreed 'to do nothing at all' for me for seven roubles a month. I should be forgiven for many sins on his account. I was drawn to such hatred at times that his very footfall would throw me into convulsions. But especially repulsive to me was his lisp. He had a tongue that was somewhat longer than is usual or something of the sort, that made him constantly lisp and hiss, and it seems he was terribly proud of this, imagining that it lent him an extraordinarily significant dignity. He spoke quietly, measuredly, with his hands behind his back, his eyes lowered towards the ground. He especially enraged me when, sometimes, he started to read from a psalter behind his partition. I endured many battles for the sake of this reading. But he passionately loved reading in the evening with a quiet, even voice, half-singing, exactly as they do for the dead. It was curious that he ended up doing just that: he is now hired to read the psalter over the deceased, and he also exterminates rats and makes shoe polish. But at that time, I couldn't sack him because it was as though he was chemically fused with my being. Furthermore, he would himself not have agreed to leave me, not in the slightest. I couldn't possibly live in *chambres garnies*:[29] my apartment was my private residence, my shell, my cave, in which I hid from the whole of humanity, and Apollon, the devil knows why, appeared to belong to this apartment, and for a whole seven years I wasn't able to drive him away.

To hold back, for example, his salary even for two, even three days, was impossible. He would have concocted such a scandal that I wouldn't have known where to put myself. But these days I was embittered towards everyone to such a degree that I decided, for some reason or another *to punish* Apollon and not to issue him his salary for the last two weeks. Long ago, about two years past, I planned to do this – if only to show him that he wouldn't dare to assert his importance over me, and that if I wanted to then I could always withhold his salary. I proposed not to speak to him about it and even stayed silent on purpose, in order to conquer his pride and force him to be the first to mention his salary. Then I would take all seven roubles from the drawer, show him that I had them and had put them aside on purpose, but that I 'didn't want, didn't want, simply didn't want to issue him his salary, I didn't want to because that's what I *did want*,' because that was 'the master's wish', because he was disrespectful, because he was a vulgarian. But if he asked me respectfully then I, perhaps, would be mollified and give it to him. Or else he would have to wait two weeks, wait three weeks, wait a whole month . . .

But as angry as I might be, he would overcome me anyway. I couldn't hold out for four days, even. He started in the way he always started in similar situations, because there had already been similar situations, trial-runs, (and I note that I knew all this in advance, I knew his despicable tactics by

heart), and this is what his tactics were: he usually started
by aiming an extraordinarily severe gaze at me, not lowering
it for several minutes in a row, especially in meeting me or
accompanying me out of the house. If, for example, I held
out and pretended that I didn't notice these stares, he would,
still silently as before, go on to the next torture. Usually,
suddenly and not for any reason, he would enter my room
quietly and smoothly while I'd be pacing or reading, and he
would stop at the door, put one hand behind his back, step a
foot forward and aim his stare at me, not just sternly but
altogether contemptuously. If I asked him, what does he need,
he answers nothing and continues to look straight at me for
another few seconds, then, somehow especially pursing his
lips, with a significant air, he slowly turns in place and slowly
goes off into his room. About two hours later he comes out
again, and again appears before me in this way. Sometimes,
in a rage, I would not even ask him: what did he need? I
would simply raise my head, sharply and imperiously, and also
start to stare straight at him. So we would stare, usually, at
each other for about two minutes; in the end he turns, slowly
and importantly, and goes off again for two hours.

If, after all this, I still wouldn't come to reason and
continued to revolt, then he would start to sigh, looking over
at me, sighing at length, deeply, as though he was measuring
the whole of my moral descent with this sigh alone, and, of
course, it all ended in the end with his total triumph: I raged,
shouted, but I was still obliged to perform that which the
matter concerned.

This time, the usual gesture of the 'severe stare' had barely
begun when I immediately lost myself in a rage and flew at him.
I was already too irritated, never mind this.

'Stand still!' I shouted in a frenzy when he slowly and

silently turned to go into his room with one hand behind his back. 'Stand still! Come back, come back, I am talking to you!' and I must have barked so unnaturally at him that he turned, with a certain amazement, even, and started to look at me. However, he continued not to say a word and this sent me mad.

'How dare you come into my room without being asked and look at me like that? Answer me!'

And, looking at me calmly for half a minute, he again started to turn around.

'Stand still!' I howled, running up to him. 'Stay where you are! So, then. Answer me now: what did you come in to look at?'

'If, momentariously, you have something to request of me then it is my duty to fulfill it,' he replied, having again kept a certain silence, lisping quietly and measuredly, raising his eyebrows and calmly tipping his head from one shoulder to the other, all the while with a horrible calmness.

'That's not what I'm on about, not at all, you hangman!' I cried, shaking with anger. 'I'll tell you, you hangman, why you come here: you can see that I am not issuing your salary, and you don't want, out of pride, to bow down and ask for it, and that's why you come here with your stupid stares, to punish me, to torment me, and you don't sus-sspect, you hangman, how stupid, stupid, stupid, stupid, stupid it is!'

He would have started to turn around again without a word but I grabbed him.

'Listen,' I shouted at him. 'Here is the money, you see, here it is!' (I pulled it out of the desk.) 'All seven roubles, but you aren't getting them – you will not get them – until such time as you come to me respectfully, with a bowed head, to ask me forgiveness. You hear?'

'That will never happen!' he responded with a kind of unnatural self-assurance.

'It will happen!' I cried. 'I give you my honest word that it will happen!'

'And there is nothing for which I should ask your forgiveness,' he continued, as though totally disregarding my cries. 'Since you here have called me a "hangman" then on that count I can have you summoned to the police station at any time for the offence.'

'Go on! Have me summoned!' I bellowed. 'Go now, this very minute, this very second! But you'll still be a hangman! Hangman! Hangman!'

But he just looked at me, then turned and, already not listening to me shouting for him to come back, went off smoothly to his room, without looking back.

If it weren't for Liza then there would have been none of this! I decided to myself. Then, having paused for a minute, importantly and solemnly but with a slow and pounding heart, I set off myself towards him, beyond the screen.

'Apollon!' I said, quietly and deliberately, but gaspingly. 'Go down, right now and hurry, don't tarry, to get the police chief!'

Meanwhile he had just sat down at his table, put on his spectacles and taken to sewing something. And, having heard my order, he snorted with laughter.

'Now, this very minute, go on! Go – or you can't even imagine what will happen!'

'You are truly out of your mind,' he remarked, not even lifting his head, lisping as slowly as before and continuing to thread his needle. 'And who has ever sent a person to go to the authorities about himself? And if you're trying to scare me – you are overstraining yourself in vain, because it won't happen.'

'Go!' I squealed, grabbing him by the shoulder. I felt that I would strike him right now.

But I didn't hear that, at that moment, the door in the front hall had opened quietly and slowly and some kind of figure had entered, stopped, and was scrutinising us in bewilderment. I glanced over, was horror-struck, and rushed into my room. There, taking hold of my hair with both hands, I leant my head against the wall and froze in that position.

About two minutes later, Apollon's slow footfall could be heard.

'Some *girl* is asking for you,' he said, staring at me especially severely, and then he stood aside and let her through – it was Liza. He didn't want to leave and watched us, mockingly.

'Leave! Leave!' I commanded him, losing myself. At that minute my clock began straining, grumbling, and then struck seven.

IX

*And into my house bold and free
As mistress of all, you shall be*

I stood before her, broken, damned, dreadfully embarrassed; and it seems I smiled, trying with all my strength to wrap myself tighter into my shaggy padded dressing gown with its flaps – well, just exactly as I had imagined to myself in a dispirited moment not long ago. Apollon left, having stood over us for a couple of minutes, but that didn't make it easier for me. The worst of all was that she was also suddenly embarrassed, to an extent that I never would have expected. At the sight of me, of course.

'Sit down,' I said, mechanically, and pulled a chair up to the table, while I sat down on the sofa. She instantly sat down, obediently, looking at me, all eyes, and obviously awaiting something from me. The naivety of this expectation was driving me into a rage but I restrained myself.

She should have tried not to notice, as if everything was normal here, but she . . . And I had the vague feeling that she would pay dearly for all this.

'You have found me in a strange situation, Liza,' I began, stammering and knowing that that was exactly not how I should have begun. 'No, no, don't think anything!' I cried out, having seen that she suddenly blushed. 'I am not ashamed of my poverty . . . On the contrary, I proudly look upon my poverty. I am poor, but noble . . . It is possible to be poor and noble,' I muttered. 'However . . . do you want tea?'

'No . . .' she started to say something.

'Wait!'

I jumped up and ran to Apollon. I really had to hide.

'Apollon,' I whispered in a feverish patter, throwing the seven roubles at him, which had remained all this time in my fist. 'Here is your salary. See, I'm issuing it. But for that you have to save me: quickly bring tea and ten rusks from the tavern. If you don't want to go then you will make an unhappy man of me! You don't know what kind of woman this is . . . This is – everything! You, perhaps, are thinking something . . . But you don't know what kind of woman this is!'

Apollon, having already sat down to his work and again put on his spectacles, did not at first put down his needle, but looked askance at the money. Then, without paying me any attention and not replying at all, continued to fuss with his thread, which he had not yet got through the needle's eye. I waited a few minutes, standing before him, with arms folded à la Napoleon.[30] My temples were moist with sweat. I was pale, and I felt it. But, thank God, he probably felt pity looking at me. Having finished with his thread, he slowly stood from his place, slowly pushed his chair back, slowly removed his spectacles, slowly counted the money and finally, asked me over his shoulder: 'Shall I take a whole portion?' And slowly walked out of the room.

While I returned to Liza, something came to my mind as I went: why not run off like this, in my dressing gown, wherever my legs may lead me, and let whatever happens, happen.

I sat down again. She looked at me with agitation. We stayed silent for several minutes.

'I will kill him!' I shouted out suddenly, banging my fist hard on the table, so much so that the ink spattered out of the inkpot.

'Ah, what do you mean!' she cried, shuddering.

'I will kill him, kill him!' I squealed, rapping on the table, in a total frenzy, and totally understanding at the same time how stupid it was to be in such a frenzy.

'You don't know, Liza, what kind of hangman he is for me. He is my hangman . . . He has now gone to get rusks. He . . .'

And suddenly I burst into tears. It was hysteria. Between sobs, I was so ashamed; but I couldn't restrain myself anymore. She was frightened.

'What's happened to you! What's happened to you!' she cried, fussing around me.

'Water, give me water – over there!' I muttered with a

FYODOR DOSTOYEVSKY

weak voice, conscious that, however, I could have very well managed without water and didn't need to mutter with a weak voice. But I was, as they say, *pretending*, for the sake of propriety, even though the hysteria had been real.

She gave me water, looking at me like a lost girl. At this moment, Apollon brought in the tea. It suddenly seemed to me that this ordinary and prosaic tea was terribly improper and miserable, after all that had passed, and I blushed. Liza looked at Apollon with fright even. He went out, not glancing at us.

'Liza, do you despise me?' I asked, staring straight at her, trembling out of impatience to know what she was thinking.

She was embarrassed and wasn't able to answer anything.

'Drink your tea!' I said spitefully. I was furious with myself, but, of course, it was always going to fall to her lot. A dreadful malice against her had boiled up suddenly in my heart. I could have killed her, it seems. In order to get my revenge on her, I silently swore not to speak one word to her the whole time. She is the cause of it all, I thought.

Our silence lasted about five minutes. The tea stood on the table. We hadn't touched it. I had got to such a point that I didn't even want to drink so that she would be even more burdened; it would have been awkward for her to take the first sip herself. Several times she looked over at me with sad bewilderment. I stubbornly stayed silent. The person to suffer most was, of course, me, because I was completely conscious of the whole loathsome meanness of my spiteful stupidity, and at the same time I couldn't restrain myself at all.

'I want . . . to get out . . . of there,' she started off, to break the silence somehow, poor thing! This was precisely what she shouldn't have spoken about at this minute, stupid as the matter was already, to a person, stupid as I am. Even my heart started to ache from pity at her clumsiness and unnecessary directness. But something ugly instantly trampled all the pity in me; in fact it egged me on even more: let everything on earth begone! Another five minutes passed.

'I haven't disturbed you, have I?' she began, timidly, barely audibly, and started to get up.

But as soon as I saw this first flash of insulted dignity, I trembled with malice so much and instantly exploded.

'What did you come here for, tell me please?' I began, gasping, not even weighing my words with logical order. I wanted to come out with it all at once, without pausing for breath. I didn't even trouble about the words with which I began.

'Why have you come? Answer me! Answer me!' I cried out, barely remembering myself. 'I will tell you, little mother, why you've come. You've come because I spoke pitiful words to you before. And now you've gone soft again and you want these "pitiful words" again. But you should know, you should know that I was laughing at you at that time. And now I am laughing at you, too. Why are you trembling? Yes, I was laughing at you! I had been insulted just before that, at dinner, by those that had come to your premises before me. I arrived at the house in order to strike one of them, an officer; but I didn't manage it, didn't find him; and so I had to take my revenge on someone, get my own back, and you turned up and I emptied my spite on you and mocked you. I was humil-iated and so I wanted to humiliate. I had been ground to a rag, and I wanted to show my power . . . That's what happened, and you thought that I had come especially to save you then, right? Is that what you thought? Is that what you thought?'

I knew that she might get confused and wouldn't under-stand the details. But I also knew that she would perfectly well understand the essence of it. And that is what happened. She went pale as a kerchief, wanted to say something, her lips distorted painfully; and it was as if she was hewn by an axe as she fell into her chair. She went on to listen to me the whole time with an open mouth, wide eyes and trembling from terrible fear. The cynicism, the cynicism of my words squashed her.

'To save you!' I continued, jumping up from my chair and running back and forth along the room before her. 'Save you from what? Yes, maybe, I am myself worse than you. Why you didn't throw it back at my chin when I read you my oration: "And you," you'd say, "why did you come here? To read a sermon?" It was power, power I needed then, I needed a game, I needed to attain your tears, humiliation, your hysterics – that is what I needed! Then I couldn't stand it myself because I am rubbish, and was frightened and the devil knows why I stupidly gave you my address. And then later, when I hadn't even reached home, I was already cursing you for all I was worth, on account of giving you this address. I already hated you because I had been lying to you. Because I like to play with words, to dream a little in my head, but in reality you know what I need: for you all to go to hell, that's what! I need peace. Yes, I would right now sell the whole world for a *kopeck* if you would all stop bothering me. Will the world go to hell, or will I not be allowed to drink my tea? I will tell you, that the world will go to hell, as long as I always get to drink my tea. Did you know this or not? Well now, I know that I am a swine, a scoundrel, an egoist, an idler. I've been trembling here these last three days out of fear that you would come. And you know what especially disturbed me these three days? It was that I had seemed such a hero before you there, and now you suddenly will see me in this ragged dressing gown, destitute and repulsive. I just finished telling you that I am not ashamed of my poverty; but you should know that I am ashamed, I am ashamed of it most of all, afraid of it above all, more than if I had stolen something, because I am so vain, it is as if I have been flayed, and even the air alone now hurts me. You must have now already guessed that I will never forgive you for the fact that you found me in my dressing gown as I was flying at Apollon like a nasty dog. The saviour, your erstwhile hero, flying at his lackey, like a mangy shaggy cur, and the latter mocking him! And those tears, just now, which I couldn't hold back in front of you, like a silly woman in shame, I will never forgive you for them! And I will also never forgive you for this confession now! Yes, you alone are to answer for everything, because you showed up, because I am a swine, because I am the most repulsive, the most silly, the most petty, the most stupid, the most envious of all the worms on the earth, none of whom are better than me, but the devil knows why, they are never embarrassed. And here I am flicked by every nit my whole life – such is my disposition. And what matter is it to me that you don't understand anything of this? And what, yes what, what matter is it to me if you perish there or not? Yes, do you understand how now, having said all this, I will hate you for the fact that you were here and you were listening? Only once in his life will a person speak his mind like this, and only in hysterics! What more do you want? What more do you want after all this, hanging around me, tormenting me, not leaving?'

But then, suddenly, a strange circumstance happened.

I was so used to thinking and envisaging everything according to books, and to imagining everything in the world as it was when I had fabricated it in my dreams before, that I didn't straight away understand this strange event. This is what happened. Liza, insulted and crushed, understood much more than I had imagined. In all of this, she had understood that which a woman always understands first of all when she loves someone in earnest: that I was myself unhappy.

The scared and insulted feeling was first replaced on her face by sorry amazement. When I started to call myself a scoundrel and a swine and my tears flowed (I had uttered this whole tirade in tears), her whole face winced with some kind of convulsion. She had wanted to stand up, to stop me; when I finished, she wasn't paying attention to my shouts of 'Why are you here, why aren't you leaving!' but to the fact that it must be very difficult for me to express all this. And she was so downtrodden, the poor thing; she considered herself to be infinitely below me; was this any time to be angry, to take offence? She suddenly jumped up from her chair with a kind of uncontainable impulse and, straining herself towards me, but still shy, and not daring to move from her place, she held her arms out to me. At that point my heart flipped. Then she suddenly threw herself at me, threw her arms around my neck and starting weeping. I also couldn't hold back and started sobbing in a way that has never before happened to me.

'No one lets me . . . I cannot be . . . kind!' I barely managed to utter, then made it to the sofa, fell onto it face down and for a quarter of an hour I sobbed with real hysterics. She pressed herself against me, hugged me and somehow froze in her embrace.

But anyway, the thing was that the hysterics had to pass. And so (I am writing the foul truth), lying face down on the sofa, having thrust my face tightly into my rotten pillow, I started bit by bit, from afar, involuntarily but irresistibly, to sense that it would now be awkward to lift my head and look Liza straight in the eye. What was I to be ashamed of? I don't know, but I was ashamed. It came into my disturbed head that our roles had now forever reversed, that the heroine was now she, and I was exactly that humiliated and crushed creature that she had been before me that night, four days ago. And all this came to me in those minutes as I lay there, face down on the sofa!

My God! Surely, I didn't envy her?

I don't know, and until now I cannot decide, but then, of course, I understood then even less than I do now. Without power and tyranny over someone, I certainly couldn't carry on. But . . . But you can't explain anything with reasoning, and therefore, there's no point in reasoning.

But I took charge of myself and lifted my head; I had to lift it up at some point. And until now, I am sure that it was because I was ashamed to look at her that suddenly another feeling sparked and flared up in my heart. It was a feeling of dominion and possession. My eyes shone with passion, and I squeezed her hands tightly. How I hated her and how I was attracted to her at that minute! One feeling strengthened the other. It almost looked like revenge! On her face a look of amazement appeared, almost fear, even, but only for a moment. She rapturously and ardently embraced me.

X

After a quarter of an hour I was running back and forth along the room in mad impatience, approaching the screen every other moment and looking through a crack in it at Liza. She was sitting on the floor, her head leaning on the bed, and was probably crying. But she didn't come out, and this bothered me. This time she knew everything already. I had insulted her definitively but . . . there's no need to talk about it. She guessed that the upsurge of my passion was namely revenge, a new humiliation for her, and also that in addition to my previous almost groundless hatred, there was now a personal, envious hatred toward her. However, I will not confirm that she understood all this distinctly; but then she totally understood that I am a person who is loathsome and, most importantly, not in any condition to love her.

I know that I will be told that this is improbable – it is improbable to be as spiteful and as stupid as I am; perhaps it will also be added that it is improbable that I wouldn't love her or at least that I didn't value her love. Why is it improbable? Firstly, I couldn't love anyone by then because, I repeat, to love for me meant to tyrannise and to morally dominate. My whole life I have never been able to imagine any other kind of love and I've reached the point that sometimes now I think that love consists of the right – voluntarily given from the beloved object – to be tyrannised. Even in my underground dreams I haven't ever imagined love as anything other than a struggle. I began it always with hatred and ended it with moral conquest, and afterwards I couldn't even imagine what to do with the conquered object. And what is so improbable about it, when I have already so succeeded in morally defiling myself, when I had become so unused to 'lively life' and had just taken it into my head to reproach and shame her with the fact that she had come to me to listen to 'pitiful words'? I didn't guess that she had not at all come in order to listen to my pitiful words but to love me, because for women, love consists of resurrection, total salvation from any kind of ruin, and regeneration, which can't manifest itself in any other way than this. However, I didn't hate her much, really, while I was running up and down the room, peeping through the crack in the screen. It was just unbearably difficult for me that she was here. I wanted her to disappear. I wanted 'peace', to be left alone in the underground. 'Lively life' had crushed me, I was so unused to it that even breathing had become hard.

But several more minutes passed and she still hadn't stood up, as though she were in oblivion. I was so unscrupulous as to quietly knock on the screen in order to remind her. She suddenly gave a start, struck up from her place and threw herself into looking for her kerchief, her hat, coat, as though she was fleeing to safety from me. After two minutes she slowly came out from behind the screen and looked at me heavily. I smirked maliciously, however, forcing myself, *for propriety's sake*, and turned away from her gaze.

'Farewell,' she uttered, making for the door.

I suddenly ran up to her, grabbed her hand, opened it and put something into it . . . and then I closed it again. Then, instantly, I turned and leapt away quickly to the other corner so that I wouldn't see, at least . . .

I wanted to lie just this minute, to write that I had done this accidentally, forgetting myself, having lost my way, like a fool. But I don't want to lie and so I will tell it straight, that I opened her hand and put something into it . . . out of spite. It came into my head to do it when I was running back and forth in my room and she was sitting behind the screens. But now I can say for certain: I did this cruelty to her, it was on purpose, it wasn't done from the heart but from my nasty head. This cruelty was so artificial, so mentally, purposefully invented, so *literary*, that I myself couldn't maintain it for minutes, even – I first leapt off into the corner in order not to see, and then with shame and despair I threw myself in pursuit of Liza. I opened the door in the hallway and started to listen.

'Liza! Liza!' I cried into the stairway, but not bravely, in half-voice.

There was no answer, it seemed to me that I heard her footsteps on the lower steps.

'Liza!' I cried louder.

No answer. But at that minute I heard from below how the outer glass door to the street slammed tight, heavily, and with a screech. A rumble ascended the stairs.

She had left. I turned back into my room in contemplation. I felt terribly burdened.

I stopped at the table by the chair on which she had been sitting, and looked in front of me vacantly. A minute or so passed and suddenly I shuddered: straight in front of me, on the table, I saw . . . in a word, I saw a rumpled, blue, five-rouble note, the same one that I had pressed into her hand a minute before. This was *that* note; it couldn't have been any other; there wasn't another in the house. She, therefore, had managed to toss it from her hand onto the table during that moment when I had leapt off into the far corner.

What now? I could have expected that she would do this. Could I have expected it? No. I was such an egoist and respected people so little, really, that I couldn't even have imagined that she would do this. I couldn't bear it. A moment later, like a madman, I rushed to get dressed, hastily throwing on whatever I could manage, and ran headlong out after her. She hadn't managed to make even two hundred paces when I ran out onto the street.

It was quiet, snow was coming down and falling almost perpendicularly, spreading like a pillow on the pavement and on the empty street. There was no one passing by, no sound to be heard. The streetlamps glimmered dolefully and redundantly. I ran about two hundred paces to the corner and stopped.

Where had she gone? And why am I running after her? Why? To fall before her, to sob in repentance, to kiss her feet, to pray for forgiveness! I wanted to do this; my whole breast was exploding into pieces, and never, never will I remember that moment with indifference. But why? I thought. 'Will I not come to hate her, perhaps even tomorrow, precisely because today I kissed her feet? Would I really give her happiness? Did I not see my own worth again today for the hundredth time? Wouldn't I torture her?

I stood in the snow, peering into the turbid darkness, and thought about this.

It would be better, wouldn't it be better, I fantasised afterwards, when already home, dampening my vivid heartache with fantasies, wouldn't it be better if she forever took this insult away with her now? An insult – it is a purification; it is the most pungent and painful consciousness! Tomorrow I would have sullied her soul with myself and exhausted her heart. But this insult now won't ever die in her, and no matter how vile the filth that awaits her, this insult will elevate and purify her . . . with hatred . . . hm . . . maybe with forgiveness. However, will all this have made it easier for her? And indeed, now I am posing myself one idle question: what is better – cheap happiness or sublime suffering? Well, which is better?

Such were my dim imaginings when I was sitting at home that evening, barely alive from the pain in my soul. Never had I endured such suffering and remorse; but could there have been even any doubt when I ran out of my quarters that I wouldn't return home having only got halfway there? Never again did I meet Liza and I heard nothing of her. I will also add that for a long time I remained satisfied with the *phrase* about the use of insult and hatred, despite the fact that I myself almost fell ill at that time from the anguish of it.

Even now, after so many years, all of this is somehow too *unpleasant* for me to remember. There is a lot that is now unpleasant to remember but . . . isn't it time to end these 'notes'? It seems to me that I made a mistake in starting to write them. At least, I have felt shame during the whole time I spent writing this *story*: consequently, this is not literature any more but corrective punishment. To tell, for example, long stories about how I deserted my life for moral depravity in a corner, from a lack of circumstances, out of estrangement from what is alive, and an arrogant malice in the underground – this is really and truly not interesting. A novel needs a hero, and here, all the characteristics of an anti-hero are collected *on purpose*; and most importantly, all this brings on an unpleasant impression because we are all unused to living, we are all crippled, each one of us more or less. We are so unused to it that we straight away feel some kind of loathing towards real 'lively life' and so we cannot stand it when we are reminded of it. We have indeed reached such a point that we almost consider real 'lively life' to be labour, almost like service, and we are all agreed among ourselves that it is better left in books. And why do we sometimes bustle about, why are we fickle, what are we looking for? We ourselves don't know what. Our lot wouldn't be worse if our capricious entreaties were fulfilled. Well, try it then – give us, for example, more independence, untie the hands of any of us, widen the circle of activity, relax custody and we . . . I can assure you, we instantly will ask to return to custody. I know that you might get angry at me, will shout at me, stamping your feet. 'Speak,' you'll say, 'for yourself alone and about your *misères* in the underground, but don't dare to speak for *all of us*.' Allow, gentlemen, that I am not trying to vindicate myself with this *all-of-us-ness*. What pertains to me personally is that which I alone have carried to extremes in my life, that which you didn't dare carry half way through, and you even took your cowardice to be prudence, and took comfort in it, lying to yourselves. And so, perhaps, I come out as more 'alive' than you. Yes, take a closer look! We don't even know where the 'lively' lives now, or what it is, what it is called. Leave us alone, without books, and we will instantly lose our way, get lost; we won't know where to attach ourselves, what to adhere to, what to love and what to hate, what to respect and what to disdain. We are even oppressed by being human, a person with a real, *individual* body and blood; we are ashamed of this, consider it a disgrace, and we strive to be some kind of imaginary pan-humans. We are stillborn infants and we have long not been born of living fathers, and this pleases us more and more. We're developing a taste for it. Soon we'll think up a way of somehow being born of an idea. Well, that's enough, I don't want to write any more 'from the underground' . . .

However, the 'notes' of this paradoxalist don't yet end. He couldn't stop himself from carrying on further. But, it also seems to us that we could stop here.

NOTES

1   This phrase was often used in critical writing of the mid-nineteenth century. It is considered to be a derivation of the phrase 'the sublime and the beautiful' from Edmund Burke's *A Philosophical Enquiry into the Origin of Our Ideas of the Sublime and the Beautiful* (1757) and Immanuel Kant's *Beobachtungen uber das Gefuhl des Schonen und Erhabenen* (1764).

2   Wagenheims. This is the name of a dentist, mentioned again later in the text.

3   *Muzhik*. A Russian peasant man.

4   *Chenapan*. This is used here as a French word, meaning rogue or rascal (originally from the German *Schnapphahn*).

5   Ge. Nikolai Nikolaievich Ge (1831-94) was a Russian realist painter

6   *Whomever It Pleases*. This refers to an article with the same title by Mikhail Yevgrafovich Saltykov-Schedrin in *Sovremmenik* (1863).

7   This is an idiom – 'he kicks out with his other knee' – which means that one reacts contrarily.

8   Stenka Razin. Stepan Timofeevich Razin was the brutal Cossack leader of a peasant rebellion in the seventeenth century.

9   This is an idiom – 'to be not even suitable as boot soles for them' – which means that one is drastically inferior to them.

10   The bird Kagan. A mythic bird of paradise.
11   Schleswig-Holstein period of man's fate. This refers to the struggle over the region of Schleswig-Holstein concerning its inclusion in either Denmark or Germany; it epitomised the problems of territory and influence in Europe.
12   The Colossus of Rhodes was a huge statue of Helios at the entrance to the harbour on the Greek island of Rhodes. It was destroyed in 226BC by an earthquake. Afanasy Anaevsky was a journalist in the mid-nineteenth century and was also apparently ill-respected.
13   This, Dostoyevsky notes, means domestic animals.
14   Pouffe. The Oxford English Dictionary traces this word to the early nineteenth century, when it described something of imitative origin. It can also refer to something that is inflated, and is certainly onomatopoeic.
15   Kostanzhoglo is a sensible landowner from Nikolai Gogol's unfinished second part of *Dead Souls*. Pyotr Ivanovich Aduyev is likewise a sensible type and he features in Ivan Goncharov's novel *An Ordinary Story*.
16   King of Spain. This likely refers to Gogol's story 'Diary of a Madman' wherein the protagonist goes mad and imagines himself to be the King of Spain.
17   *Vershok*. A unit of measurement equivalent to 4.445 cm. In the nineteenth century, height was often described in *vershok* and *arshin* (71.12cm) but two *arshin* were assumed in the measurement so only the additional *vershok* were mentioned. Here, therefore, the officer is about 187cm in height.
18   *Grivennik*. A ten-*kopeck* silver coin.
19   *Misère*. This, as Dostoyevsky notes, means poverty, destitution.
20   *Superflu*. From the French, meaning superfluous, but the inference here is something like 'crème de la crème'.
21   *Bon ton*. This, as Dostoyevsky notes, means in good taste.

22 Gostiny Dvor. A covered arcade of shops in St Petersburg on Nevsky Prospect.

23 Manfredian. This refers to the hero of Lord Byron's dramatic poem *Manfred* who is jaded and proud, having sold his soul to the devil.

24 *Droit du seigneur*. From the French; the right of a feudal lord to take a serf's new bride and spend the wedding night with her.

25 *Poltinnik*. Fifty *kopecks*.

26 *Silence*. This is given in French in Dostoyevsky's original text with a translation of the word as a footnote.

27 *Grosh*. In the nineteenth century, a *grosh* was worth half a *kopeck*.

28 *And into my house bold and free, As mistress of all, you shall be*. Lines from the poem by Nekrasov used as an epigraph to Part Two of this novel.

29 *Chambres garnies*. This, as Dostoyevsky notes, means furnished rooms.

30 *À la Napoleon*. This, as Dostoyevsky notes, means in the style of Napoleon.

A NOTE ON THE TYPE

Goudy Old Style was designed by Frederic W. Goudy in 1915. It is a graceful, slightly eccentric typeface, and is prized by book designers for its elegance and readability.

Inspired by William Morris' Arts and Crafts movement, Frederic Goudy designed over ninety typefaces throughout his career, and is one of the most influential American type designers of the twentieth century.

ABOUT THE TYPE